The CEO Can Drop Dead
A That's Not Romance Novel
By
Moira J. Moore

Published by Moira J. Moore
Copyright 2015 Moira J. Moore

Dedicated to the survivors of all forms of abuse.

A portion of the author's royalties is donated to organisations working with survivors of abuse.

Chapter One

It was Friday afternoon and Catherine Aherne was on her laptop. She had broken one of her own rules, damn it, and had let her gaze slide down to the comments below a news article. She closed her eyes and pinched the bridge of her nose. "Do not respond to idiots online. Do not respond to idiots online. Do not - "

Her phone rang. The number displayed belonged to Fast Act, one of the four temp agencies that gave Catherine work. She pressed the phone on. "Hello, this is Catherine Aherne."

"This is Sara from Fast Act. I might have a job for you."

Sara. That was a new one. Fast Act had the highest turnover rate of any place of work Catherine had ever dealt with as an employee, as a client, or as a customer. She didn't know what kind of stress came with filling positions, but the rate of burnout seemed even higher than that among social workers, and that was saying something. "When does it start?"

"Monday."

Of course. Who needed notice? Fortunately, there were no trips to Europe to cancel. "What's the job?"

"It's for a computer software company called Create and Conquer. They need someone to organise emails."

OK. Boring. And 'conquer.' That didn't sound promising. "What's the rate?"

"Twenty dollars an hour."

They could get a high school student to do it for minimum wage, but she wasn't complaining.

"It's expected to take about six weeks."

It was good timing. Her current manuscript was in the hands of her editor, leaving her with no pressing deadlines, and her book sales were hitting a bit of slump on Amazon. "I can do that."

"Great. I'll scan you the paperwork. Please sign it and send it back to me as quickly as possible."

"Will do." As Sara hung up, Catherine googled Create and Conquer.

A relatively new company, started in 2009, employing over forty people and doing quite well, with annual profits in the tens of millions. Expected to do great things. Praise for its innovation. Awards for being one of the best places to work in Ontario, which didn't mean much if one didn't know the parameters being used. Likely to be a major player in the future.

It was downtown. One hour of driving and the hell of Ottawa construction.

Ah well.

She went to the kitchen to pour herself a glass of white wine. When she returned to her computer, the lure of the comment section had been broken. She followed a Facebook link to a YouTube video of yet another cover of *Uptown Funk.*

Chapter Two

The business Catherine was already referring to as C and C was on the top floor of a twenty-two storey building smack in the middle of downtown Ottawa. Which meant that a day of parking would eat most of an hour's pay. Still, she was better off than a lot of people who had to work downtown, struggling on the viciously low minimum wage. And at least she didn't have to rely on the busses. She liked to show up at work on time.

She filed through the revolving door with all of the other suits, but she went to the reception desk instead of the elevators. She smiled at the security guard. "Hello. I'm Catherine Aherne and I'm expected by Create and Conquer on the twenty-second floor."

He nodded and picked up a phone receiver, pressing one of a long list of lights on the base. After a moment, he said into the receiver, "There's someone down here waiting for someone." After another moment, he said, "Thanks," and he hung up. "Someone will be down in a minute."

"Thank you," she said, hiding her horror at the lax security. He hadn't even given them her name.

She stood by the wall, out of everyone's way, where she could watch for someone coming out of one of the six elevators instead of going in. They were all hurrying, hurrying, hurrying, mostly frowning, carrying travel mugs and briefcases. She didn't know how people did it, month after month, year after year. It had been driving her crazy.

It wasn't long before one person slid out of an elevator and avoided getting crushed back in by the crowd. She wasn't carrying any kind of bag, not even a purse, so Catherine assumed she was the person from C and C. Catherine stepped forward and waved.

The woman smiled at her. "Catherine Aherne?"

"Yes. Hello."

The woman held out her hand. "I'm Sandy Howell. I'm the HR agent."

'Agent.' Interesting choice of word.

Catherine shook her hand. "Pleasure to meet you, Sandy."

"It's great that you're early. I can give you a bit of a tour before you meet Lance."

"Lance as in Lance MacCallan, the CEO?"

"Yes, but we're all on a first name basis. Formality is so stifling to creativity."

That was encouraging.

"We have to use this elevator." Sandy pointed. "It's the only one that goes all the way to the top."

They shoved their way in. The elevator had reflective surfaces on all sides. All the better for everyone to see what everyone else was doing. Many of the occupants swiped a white card, the size of a credit card, over a scanner under the panel of buttons before pressing their floor, and Sandy did the same.

"Nice weather, isn't it?" Sandy asked.

Time for chitchat. "Very warm for mid-September," Catherine agreed.

"Do you think we'll have a winter as bad as the last one?"

Catherine had no idea. "I hope not. My skin still hasn't recovered from the wind chill."

Damn, they had a lot of floors to stop at. And, of course, there were always those who couldn't just get off and go. They had to put one foot over the threshold and then pause to chat a little bit more to whomever they were leaving behind.

Catherine wondered if anyone had ever been strangled for doing that.

"I did a little research about Create and Conquer online," she said. As long as they had time to kill, it didn't hurt to let an employee of the company know that she was showing an interest. "Very impressive."

Sandy grinned, her eyes lighting up. "I know! We're doing really well, and everything is looking good. Except - " She halted her words, glancing at the few others still in the elevator. "It's a great place to work. You're going to love it."

It would have to be an absolutely fabulous place to work in order to make Catherine love arranging emails, but it was nice to know that it would be a positive working environment. That was what made or broke a job. "I like the sound of it already."

They finally reached the twenty-second floor, the only ones remaining in the elevator. The elevator opened into a reception area that stretched from the right side of the building all the way to the left, a long narrow strip with huge windows on either end. The window on the right end had a glass door, and Catherine could see a balcony beyond it.

A balcony at twenty-two storeys. Neat.

The walls were painted a light grey. Black leather couches were set near the windows. No doubt very hot in the summer. The modern art on the walls probably meant something to people who knew something about art, but in shades of white, black, and grey, with no other colours, it didn't do anything to warm the stark environment. A glass shelf held a dozen industry awards. Catherine wasn't close enough to read what they were for, but she imagined they reflected the praise the company had received online.

If people needed to be escorted to the floor, why did the company have a reception area? Did they often bring someone up and then make them wait? Was it for show? Was the HR person the one who always collected them? It seemed a strange procedure.

A glass wall divided the reception area from the rest of the floor. Two large glass doors were to the side of the receptionist, whose desk was nothing more than a black slab of glass – or plastic? – supported by four slightly curving grey steel legs. The receptionist had a landline, a computer monitor, a keyboard, and the smallest hard drive Catherine had ever seen. That was it. No paper, no photos, nothing personal.

"Catherine," said Sandy, "this is Nancy. Nancy, Catherine is going to be helping us out for a few weeks."

Nancy smiled. "Hi, Catherine. Welcome aboard."

"Thank you. I'm looking forward to starting. I've heard good things about the company." Always show enthusiasm.

"You'll love it. It's great."

Two friendly faces was a good start. "Are we allowed to use the balcony?"

"Only when one of the bosses is supervising, unfortunately. Insurance issues. But we have office lunches out there pretty often."

Catherine hoped they would have one while she was there. From what she could see, the view was fantastic.

Another scanner had been fixed into the glass wall beside one of the glass doors. Sandy swiped her card over the scanner. After the scanner buzzed, Sandy opened the door and waved Catherine through it.

In contrast to the darkness of the reception area, the space beyond the glass partition was so bright it was almost painful. Lots of windows, few solid walls. Either their electricity costs were through the roof or everyone cooked in the summer and froze in the winter.

Catherine realised the company was one of those open concept deals. The space was a long rectangle, taking up the entire storey. On the left side, right next to the partition to the reception area, there was a door in what looked like a slab of grey concrete. After that, a line of offices surrounded by nothing more than walls of glass. Some of the glass had writing on it, written from the inside. Evidence of brainstorming. More offices lined the far end of the floor, also with glass walls. The wall along the right side of the floor was grey concrete, with no windows, and it looked grim and almost oppressive in comparison. It had a door-less opening that revealed to Catherine what looked like a hallway running along the length of the floor on the other side of the wall, and a window.

Down the middle of the floor, there were two grey tables about a metre and a half wide and eight metres long. Eight desktop computers were on each table, about a metre apart, alternating from side to side. As far as Catherine could see, no one was using them. There was no detritus around the keyboards, and only one lonely chair at the computer closest to the door.

Between the other end of the long tables and the offices were five smaller tables, round, accommodating six people each and covered with computers and paperwork. Two white boards stood at the left side, covered with diagrams and notes Catherine couldn't read. There were twenty-five people gathered there, many mingling and chatting, a handful already at work at their computers.

Out of twenty-five people, three were women.

It was obviously one of those organisations that believed people worked best when they were piled on top of each other. Catherine could see three employees wearing noise cancelling headphones. She'd have to bring her pair in from home the next day.

A basketball net was nailed to the right wall. All well and good to encourage people to play at work, but she wouldn't be able to concentrate through a noisy basketball game.

"This is my office," Sandy said, pointing at the door in the concrete slab to the left. "It's the only one people can't see into." She opened the door and firmly closed it once she and Catherine were in the room. "We want people to know that they can speak here and their privacy will be protected."

Catherine didn't point out that protecting people's identity while they were in the office wasn't very effective when everyone else could see them coming and going. It was none of her business.

"Please, have a seat."

The office was the most cluttered part of the twenty-second floor that Catherine had seen so far. An ugly, solid grey desk with drawers in it and covered with files, black filing cabinets, and a table with a photocopier. She supposed that because it was out of everyone's sight, it could be functional instead of stylish.

Catherine wondered if Sandy felt cut off and isolated from the others, or if she enjoyed the seclusion.

Sandy took a file from one of the cabinets and opened it on her desk. It was thin. Catherine knew it held her documentation from Fast Act and a copy of her CV. "Before we get started, I'm going to have to get you to sign a non-disclosure agreement. I'm sorry, it's necessary for this kind of business."

"Not at all. It's standard." Catherine accepted the agreement and read it quickly. It was poorly drafted and she could have told Sandy about the gaping holes in it that should be filled, but that wasn't why she was there. She signed and dated it. "Can I have a copy of that, please?"

"Oh," Sandy said, surprised. "Sure." She photocopied the agreement.

Catherine folded the copy and put it in her purse.

Sandy opened the top drawer in her desk and took out a white security card. "This will get you onto the floor and into the office whenever you need."

"Oh, you're -" *going to give a temp you didn't even interview yourself unfettered access to your office* – "Thank you."

"While most of us do have an idea about why you're here, Lance would prefer you didn't talk about it to anyone."

"Of course."

"If you have any concerns or difficulties or questions, anything at all, you can come to me. I'm here to help you and what you say won't go beyond these four walls."

That was what all HR people said. It was quaint. As though Catherine wasn't fully aware that HR worked on behalf of the management, not the employees.

"Do you have any questions right now?" Sandy asked.

"Nope. I'm good." Catherine felt she had demonstrated sufficient enthusiasm for C and C and didn't need to waste anyone's time with unnecessary inquiries.

"Great. Then I'll show you around."

The first thing Sandy did once they were out of her office was point at the single chair at the end of the long table on the left side of the floor. "We're putting you there."

Oh, thank god.

"We're not being anti-social or trying to make you feel unwelcome," Sandy added apologetically. "It's just that they're all working on confidential stuff."

"I understand," Catherine assured her, wondering why the confidential stuff wasn't being hidden behind proper walls. "And if it makes you feel any better, I wouldn't understand anything I heard or saw anyway."

Sandy smiled. "Me neither," she confessed. She waved her hand in a circular motion Catherine assumed was meant to indicate the open middle of the floor. "They refer to that as the bullpen. Everyone watches too many police procedurals."

"I'm a TV fiend myself."

"This is the way to the lunchroom and the washrooms."

Catherine followed Sandy to the door-less entrance on the right side of the floor, taking a sharp left immediately after. It was not a hall but a long, narrow room. She and Sandy passed a ping pong table, an air hockey table, three arcade games, and a card table covered with nerf ball guns to get to the kitchen area on the left side of the room. The kitchen included a fridge, a dishwasher, cabinets, a sink, three microwaves, and three enormous coffee makers. Squeezed into the right side of the room were two long high tables that might accommodate about ten people each and six smaller round tables. The washrooms, one for men and one for women, were at the end of the room.

"Anyone can drink the coffee," said Sandy. "We ask that everyone clean up after themselves and leave each other's food alone."

The kitchen looked clean right then, but it was early in the morning.

Catherine put her uninspired salad in the fridge, hoping no one would steal it. There was a food court on the main floor of the building, but the prices were too high for her to manage every day of the week.

"I'll take you to Lance's office now. He and a few of the others are having a meeting."

A meeting. That sounded a little intimidating. It would probably feel like being interviewed by many people at once, something she had experienced in the past but not an experience she cared to have repeated.

Lance's office was in the far left corner of the floor, larger than all of the other offices. It was, like all of the others, surrounded by walls of transparent glass. Set directly into the corner, it was shaped like an L. Catherine could see exercise equipment in the left side of the L: a stationary bike, a bench and rack, free weights and bars. Lance worked all hours, then. A black glass desk was angled across the back corner, which meant when he sat at it Lance would have his back to the enormous windows and the fantastic view of Ottawa that they offered. Two chairs were set in front of the desk. In the right side of the L, a fourth chair faced two small couches, one set against the back wall, the second against the glass wall that the office shared with the office next door.

A man sat in the chair, four more and one woman in the two couches. No one wore a suit. Catherine felt overdressed.

The glass door was open, and Sandy stood beside it to announce, "Hello, everyone, this is Catherine from the temp agency."

"Hello, Catherine," said the man seated in the chair. He had an appealing deep voice. "Take a seat. Thank you, Sandy."

Sandy nodded and closed the door after Catherine entered the office. Catherine took the empty seat at the end of the couch against the glass wall.

"Welcome, Catherine. I'm Lance."

Wasn't he the handsome one? Even though he was seated, she could tell he was tall, with nice broad shoulders and a trim form. Jawline firm enough for a comic book superhero, dark blue eyes, short black hair. About mid-thirty, with the tanned skin of someone who spent a lot of time outdoors. Yes, he would be a nice slice of scenery.

He was wearing a plain red t-shirt, black capris, and sandals. Catherine had never been in an office environment that had people walking around like that.

"This is Seth." Lance nodded at the man seated closest to him, in the couch set against the back wall.

Seth, the only one with silver in his hair, smiled at her. "Hello, Catherine." He wore blue jeans, green Converse sneakers, and a light cream-coloured sweater.

"Hello."

"Adam," Lance continued.

Adam was a rotund young man wearing proper trousers and a button shirt. At least Catherine's clothing wasn't too freakish for these people.

"Steve."

Steve looked barely twenty and Catherine didn't know what message he was trying to convey by wearing an honest to god Grateful Dead t-shirt. Did he even know who they were? Was he truly a fan? Was he trying to be ironic?

"David."

David seemed to be embracing the stereotype of a computer geek while trying to inspire a war between two science fiction franchises with his shirt. *Live long and carry a lightsaber.*

"Samantha."

Samantha appeared to be near thirty, and she wore black jeans and a Hello Kitty t-shirt.

No one was giving Catherine titles, any indication of what their positions in the company might be.

As they exchanged their greetings, Catherine took a small notebook and a pen out of her purse.

Lance left his chair to take a paper file off his desk, and he held it out to Catherine. "We have been developing software for a new online social networking site," he said, returning to his chair as Catherine opened the file. "We call it In-Ect, and we've been looking for financing for it for the past two years."

Catherine didn't understand why a software company the size of C and C would need outside financing, but that sort of thing wasn't within her scope of knowledge or experience.

Did the world really need another online social networking site?

"If we can launch the site, it could mean billions of dollars for us."

Catherine was in the wrong business.

"Five years ago, we were consulting with another software company, Under-Ware."

She found the name on the first page in the file and held back a wince at the spelling. She hated puns.

"They lost interest in the project, so we continued to work on it alone. Then, three months ago, Under-Ware released an online social networking site called Circle Route, to huge acclaim."

Catherine hadn't heard of it, but she tended to be in the same arena as grandparents when it came to online trends. She still wasn't sure what Snapchat was about and she'd never been interested enough to find out.

"Circle Route is almost exactly what we have planned for In-Ect, and we suspect Under-Ware is using software developed from what we shared with them. Unfortunately, we don't have any written agreements about the consultation or any evidence that designs were revealed to them. All we have to prove that we worked with them is whatever is in our emails from that time."

Ah. She was getting it. Bad non-disclosure agreement, no consultation agreement. It was stupid, but she'd seen a lot of companies begin with weak legal documents and stumble along successfully until it all blew up in everyone's face.

"We need you to go through every email sent and received by everyone in this company for the last five years, looking for references to the software."

It took great effort on Catherine's part to keep her mouth from dropping open in dismay. Five years multiplied by all of the C and C employees that had come and gone.

"We've given you a list of Under-Ware employees that were part of the discussions, so you'll be able to narrow the outside recipients down to those, but you'll need to read everything that was sent within C and C. Even emails that weren't sent to Under-Ware's employees may refer to them and give us ideas about relevant meetings or phone calls that might have occurred."

Ok, limiting the recipients cut back on the enormity of the task. A little.

"You will have access to all of those emails, but many of them have been stored in archives that make current search functions a little clumsier. We never expected to have to do something like this. And you won't be able to just search the names because there's no telling how individuals might have described the software. You'll have to read everything."

Joy. 'Who stole my sandwich?' 'Why am I the only one making coffee?' 'Put your dirty dishes in the dishwasher. Your mother doesn't work here.'

"We've hired a lawyer to help us with this, but we obviously don't want to pay her a thousand dollars an hour to slog through tens of thousands of emails."

Tens of thousands of emails.

"Her name and contact information are in the file. Once you have a grasp on what's in the emails, you can ask her how she wants the information organised, but don't contact her too often, or waste her time. Again, a thousand dollars an hour."

At that rate, she had to be a Toronto lawyer.

"The file has the password to the computer you'll be using, the email address we've set up for you, and instructions on how to open the archives. Do you think you can handle this?"

She closed the file and looked at him. There was something a little off about his tone, a slight edge. "Yes, of course."

"You were a lawyer."

That came out of nowhere, and it meant he had either read her CV or asked Sandy about it. Did he not trust Sandy to do her job, or was he a hands-on person in general? "Yes."

"And now, you're a ... temp."

There was no mistaking the contempt with which he used the word, as if it was something inherently filthy.

She straightened in her seat. "Yes, I am."

"Couldn't cut it as a lawyer?"

No, she decided she'd rather write books. Which meant she needed to work as a temp to supplement her income. But she wasn't going to go into that. He would only sneer at her for her failure as a writer, probably one of those people who thought success in writing meant making a fortune. And if he found out she was self-published, well, who knew where it would go from there? Not a real writer, then. Maybe some rant about self-publishing being the end of civilisation.

Besides, she didn't need to defend herself. "No."

She didn't know what they – him and the silent audience observing the scene - expected from her. To be flustered, to try to reassure everyone that she was competent, maybe even cry. But she had none of that to give them. She'd worked with bullies before.

Call-Me-Lance seemed to be waiting for more from her. When she said nothing, he added, "Find a way to impress me by the end of the day. So far, I haven't seen anything."

That was her dismissal from the meeting. In silence, she put the notebook and the pen back into her purse, rose from the couch with her purse in her right hand and the file in her left, and escaped from the office, closing the door behind her.

What an ass.

There were many who had no respect for temps. It was part of the job.

She walked back to the other end of the bullpen and sat in the chair Sandy had pointed out. She turned on the computer, and as she waited for it to boot up, she wrote in her notebook:

Monday, September 14, 2015
Arrived approximately 8:37 am.

Met Sandy Howell of human resources, who had me sign a non-disclosure agreement and gave me a security card to the building and the office. Meeting with Lance MacCallan, CEO, Seth [NAME], Adam [NAME], Steve [NAME], David [NAME], and Samantha [NAME]. After providing the instructions concerning my job, MacCallan, with no provocation on my part, attempted to humiliate me in front of the others by asking me about my past as a lawyer, suggesting I "couldn't cut it," and implying I was incompetent.

Having lowered her expectations about how pleasant the work environment was going to be, Catherine read the notes about Circle Route and In-Ect. They seemed completely different to her, Circle Route kind of like Facebook and In-Ect kind of like YouTube, but trying to determine whether C and C actually had a case was not her job.

Catherine opened the archives. Tens of thousands of emails, from September 1, 2010 to September 4, 2015. A jumbled mess, not organised in any way, not even by name. She wasn't sure she would be able to read them all in six weeks.

From the most recent emails, she got the full names and titles of the people in that fiasco of a meeting. Seth Adda, CFO and an original partner. Adam Bell, software development manager. Steve Hooks, senior developer. He seemed young for that, but what did she know? David Pine, regular old boring IT. Samantha Kelly, quality assurance analyst.

What was the best way to tackle the enormous task? Starting at the earliest email and working her way through to the most recent one would be ridiculous. She would never be able to keep track of who said what. She'd have to make notes of everything she did and that would take forever.

She'd need to organise them before reading them.

By recipient?

No, by sender. Create folders for each of the C and C senders – ugh – and then start reading them. Create new folders for the emails that actually made references to the software and to Under-Ware. Then, create an index and maybe some summaries in a separate Word document. Yeah, that made sense.

She started the gargantuan task of creating close to one hundred folders, representing employees past and present, and clicking and dragging emails to them. Her environment faded from her mind.

She was startled when someone suddenly appeared at her side. "Excuse me."

Catherine jumped and looked up. Samantha. She glanced at the time on the computer monitor. A little over an hour had passed.

Samantha looked about the room, then bent down a little. "You'll have to forgive Lance," she said in a low voice.

Catherine raised an eyebrow. Did she?

"Patrick Dale – he's one of the names on the list – he and Lance were friends. Close friends. So this betrayal, it's not just about the money. It's deeper than that."

Catherine knew she should pretend to accept that justification, but MacCallan's behaviour had been vile, and she resented being told she should excuse him without an apology from him. "The fact that he's angry at one person means it's ok to jump down someone else's throat? In front of other people?"

Samantha's eyebrows rose in disbelief. Catherine had no doubt the other woman had expected a response along the lines of *Sure, no problem.*

"Not ok," Samantha said, "but forgivable."

"And if he apologises, I'll forgive him." If he was sincere. And if the apology was delivered in front of the same people he'd used as an audience for his insults.

Samantha straightened, her posture stiffening and her eyes narrowing. "We all get along here," she said coolly. "It's essential for encouraging creativity."

Catherine raised her hands, palms out. "I'm just a temp. I'm not interested in trying to change the work culture."

Without another word, Samantha stormed off.

"Oh, this is going to be a fun six weeks," Catherine muttered.

Chapter Three

At 1:32, Catherine logged off her computer and headed to the lunchroom, where she found, to her disappointment, Call-Me-Lance seated at one of the round tables with Adam and two young men from the bullpen. So Call-Me-Lance liked to mingle with the plebes.

Those with him seemed relaxed, seemed to enjoy his company. If C and C was a genuinely collaborative, respectful work environment, why had Call-Me-Lance gone after her?

Maybe he was leery of new people after the alleged betrayal by Patrick. Maybe Catherine was going through some form of hazing. Maybe he was so baffled by the idea of someone quitting law to become a temp that he didn't know what to do with himself.

None of those reasons justified his behaviour, but she couldn't help being curious.

To her relief, her lunch was still in the fridge, and apparently untouched. She took it to the table farthest from the men. As she had no interest in overhearing conversations she wasn't a part of, she popped earbuds into her ears and turned the volume of her iPod up high. She took her Kobo out of her purse so she could read while she picked at her boring salad. She knew she would look anti-social, but it had been her experience that few were interested in interacting with temps.

She cut her lunch short. She was entitled to an hour, but she didn't want to be around Call-Me-Lance any more than necessary. It was bad enough having to pass by his table to get a cup of coffee, still listening to her iPod to dissuade anyone there from talking to her. She continued to bop along to Beyoncé until she got back to her computer and jumped back into search, click, and drag.

Nearly two hours later, she was surprised when Seth stopped by. "We didn't get a chance to talk earlier," he said with a slight accent she couldn't quite identify. Welsh? "Do you have everything you need?"

Caught a little flatfooted by his friendly demeanour, Catherine said, "Uh, yes. I think so. Thank you."

"Where did you go to law school?"

They weren't going to talk about Call-Me-Lance's behaviour. Ok. As long as Seth didn't try to justify it, she was fine with that. "Queen's."

He smiled. "My daughter started at Queen's this year."

Ah, nostalgia. "What's she taking?"

"Engineering."

"Will she be buying a school jacket and dyeing it purple?"

"I imagine she'll be getting into every ritual she hears of. She got to the top of the greased pole."

"Congratulations!" Catherine kept to herself what she thought of the psychology behind having what was once a solely masculine department climbing a greased pole during orientation.

"Yeah, she was pretty pleased."

Catherine had skipped most of orientation, preferring to go drinking with the five people she had met in the first hour. Except for the law faculty's BBQ. It had been held on the strip of land between the Kingston Penitentiary and the yacht club, and she had gone simply because she couldn't believe anyone would put a yacht club right beside one of Canada's oldest prisons.

On one side of their picnic, a tall grim nineteenth century stone wall, with some of Canada's most notorious criminals within. On the other, the pretty little boats of the well-off bobbing on the waves of Lake Ontario. Between them, a hundred and fifty future lawyers eating hamburgers and throwing Frisbees. Surreal.

It wouldn't be the same for the new crop of students. The penitentiary was closed.

"I have to get back," Seth said. "I just wanted to say a proper hello."

"Thank you," Catherine responded with sincerity. "I appreciate it." It was always nice to know there were decent people about, though she imagined she wouldn't be interacting with Seth much.

No one else spoke to her until 5:09, when she logged out.

"What have you accomplished?" a voice boomed behind her.

She jumped in her swivel chair. She imagined that was a minor boost to Call-Me-Lance's ego.

She turned her chair around and looked up at him. Way up. He was standing too close in a blatant attempt to intimidate her.

He was nowhere near as scary as Judge Karr. Lawyers with over thirty years of experience would suddenly agree to adjournments, for the flimsiest of reasons, if it meant escaping the vicious temper of Judge Karr. "I have been organising the emails into folders according to sender."

He barely let the words leave her mouth before demanding, "How many have you read?"

"None, yet."

"None?" He seemed genuinely appalled.

"I have always found it more efficient to do some preliminary organisation when dealing with large amounts of information."

"And, of course, you are paid by the hour," he sneered.

Ass. "I can give you a written report providing you with the number of emails in the archives, the number of senders, how many -"

"I don't have time to read meaningless reports," he snapped. "And I don't want you spending time we're paying for to write them. Do better tomorrow." He stalked off to the back of the floor. To his office, she supposed.

Catherine managed to resist giving his back the finger. It wasn't wise in the open concept environment, where others might see her. Besides, when she flipped someone off she preferred to do it to their face.

She wrote in her notebook:

At 5:09, MacCallan stopped by my table, crowded too close to me, asked what I had done today, brushed off my offer of a written report, indicated he was unsatisfied with what I had done, and told me to do better tomorrow.
Left office approximately 5:13.

And she escaped.

The drive home was as stressful as Ottawa rush hour usually was.

She sighed with relief when she was finally in her apartment. It was a very small one-bedroom. She'd had to get rid of her furniture when she moved, most of it couldn't fit, and what she'd replaced it with was inherited from friends and relatives, picked up at yard sales, or IKEA. The layout of the apartment wasn't great, it had no balcony, and it was cramped, but she was comfortable enough. The building was clean and quiet, and the superintendents were friendly and hard-working. The dingy exercise room on the first floor spared her the cost of a gym membership. The coin washers and dryers in the basement were cheap.

It would do until she could afford a waterfront condo in Kingston.

Grimacing at the thought of exercising, she changed into shorts and a t-shirt and went down to the first floor to spend half an hour taking her frustrations out on the elliptical machine. After returning to her apartment and showering, she sat at her laptop with a bowl of reheated stir fry and a glass of white wine, her calm restored.

She smiled when she saw that she'd gotten an email from Barry Odjig. Her ex. They'd had to split when he got a job offer in B.C. He'd asked her to go with him, but they hadn't even been living together at that point. She hadn't thought it a good idea, combining the stress of moving in together with the stress of moving to a different part of the country. She loved Vancouver, but she hadn't been prepared to leave Ontario on a permanent basis.

She hadn't been prepared to share living space, either. The one time she'd lived with a boyfriend, it had been less than four months before she wanted to kill him. It hadn't been his fault; he'd been a perfectly nice guy. It was more likely hers; the stress of being a first year lawyer hadn't made her a fun person to be around. Still, the negative experience had left her leery of trying it again.

She and Barry had flared into the worst arguments of their relationship and they'd stopped speaking for a week, but after they'd both calmed down, Barry got excited about the move, and Catherine promised never to use him as a character in a book. They'd developed a genuine friendship. Almost a year later, they were still exchanging emails. He loved his job, loved Vancouver, and Catherine had been getting the feeling, from little hints here and there, that he was seeing someone.

She hoped he wasn't afraid to tell her. There would be a bit of a sting over being replaced – they'd dated for almost two years – but he was a wonderful person and he deserved happiness wherever he could find it.

Her phone rang. Lina Cheung. Best friend and favourite drinking partner. Catherine tapped the phone on. "Hey there."

"How did it go?" Lina demanded.

"The work is dead boring and the boss is a total ass."

"Really?"

"Total. Ass."

"What did he do?"

"Insulted me in front of a bunch of strangers." She shouldn't have brought it up. She was getting tense again.

"What did he say?"

"It doesn't matter. I've had worse." Many of the lawyers at the firm she'd articled at had seemed to take special joy in making the students feel like trash.

"Do you want to go out for shooters?"

Very much. "I don't think showing up hungover is a good idea."

"*Space Drive Five* is coming out this Friday. Do you want to go? It looks like it will be really bad, and we can get drunk after."

"Yeah. That sounds good." But Friday seemed so far away. "Let's talk about your life for a while. Academic politics are much more interesting than learning there is yet another obnoxious employer in the world. Any news on the grant?"

"Oh, you mean the one no one wants to give for research in gender studies?" Lina asked sarcastically. "I don't want to talk about it. Let's talk about the fact that you should be taking busses to work."

Catherine rolled her eyes. "I'm not taking busses until they're reliable." And wouldn't stretch her one-hour commute into something closer to two. "End of story."

"You want to bash Stephen Harper?"

"Now you're cooking."

Chapter Four

Tuesday, September 15, 2015
Arrived approximately 8:24 am.
Lunch from 12:38 to 1:16.
MacCallan came to my table at 4:58 to ask about my
progress, brushed off attempts to provide details, and
expressed dissatisfaction with my work. He stood
too close to my chair.
Left approximately 5:27 pm.

Chapter Five

Wednesday, September 16, 2015
Arrived approximately –

"I've seen you writing in that several times," Seth said, and what was it about people sneaking up on her? "What are you doing? Not collecting information for the enemy, I hope." He winked at her.

She laughed. "No. I like to keep track of the exact hours I work. I had a dispute with a different temp agency about the hours I reported, and I'm hoping keeping a diary will make it easier to prove my case if it happens again." No, that had never happened. One of the best pieces of advice her father had ever given her was to keep a daily record of every job she'd ever had. She hadn't been too rigorous about it while working retail, and she hadn't suffered for it, but once she had started working in offices, she'd made a daily habit of it.

"That's the lawyer in you, I suppose."

That, too. "Some lessons you never forget."

He smiled and wandered off to the lunchroom.

Catherine finished her notes and logged in.

Like the two days before, few people talked to her. They worked at their end of the bullpen and went to the lunchroom and washrooms via their side of the floor. The four people who had offices along the left side of the floor, between Sandy's office and Call-Me-Lance's, never introduced themselves to her and gave her vague smiles if their gazes happened to meet.

Catherine didn't mind working in solitude, usually, but arranging emails into folders was one of the most boring things she had ever done, and that included photocopying case law for hours. She had no ethical objections to people taking mini-breaks and checking their email, doing a little internet surfing, she thought it increased productivity, but her computer monitor was large and anyone passing by could see what she was doing. Looking at her phone would send the same message. She didn't want to give anyone, a.k.a. Call-Me-Lance, any ammunition to use against her. So all she could do was search, click, and drag.

She kept an eye out for Call-Me-Lance. He had entered the lunchroom at about 1:00 the day before, and she had been in there. She had lingered a further fifteen minutes out of defiance, she didn't want him thinking he could intimidate her, but she was happy to avoid his company whenever she could, and she wanted to learn his routine so she could work around it.

Search, click, drag.

She wondered if the damage the tedium was doing to her brain was worth the money.

Be grateful for the money. Be grateful for the money. Be grateful for the money.

Call-Me-Lance headed to the lunchroom at 1:06.

Maybe it was time to start looking for a real, full-time job. Something that would keep her mind going. Something with benefits.

Benefits! Ha!

She could go back to being a lawyer. She'd kept up her licence.

No.

Search, click, drag.

A permanent full-time job would rob her of any time to write. She would have to squeeze her passion and her sanity into the weekends, in between grocery shopping, vacuuming – sometimes – and reassuring her friends and family that she wasn't dead.

And there wasn't really such a thing as a permanent job anymore. Unless she got herself appointed to the Senate.

She would be a good senator. She'd show up, for one thing. And she would actually read the bills before voting on them.

Maybe she'd register with the Liberal party. There was still time before the election.

She closed her eyes, corralling her thoughts. Despite the monotony of the work, she did need to give her attention to it.

Call-Me-Lance left the lunchroom and went straight back to his office at 2:09.

It was a little later than she liked for lunch, but she preferred to eat later than too early. She logged off her computer, contemplating the salad that was waiting for her with little enthusiasm.

Sandy was the only one in the lunchroom, dividing her garbage among the three recycling bins. She smiled. "Catherine. How's it going?"

"Fine."

"No problems?"

Aside from the boss being a jerk? "None at all. What I'm doing is fairly simple."

"There's going to be pizza brought in tomorrow. We do it every Thursday, bring in pizza or sandwiches for everyone. You're welcome to join us."

"Thank you. I might do that." *No way in hell.*

Sandy left and Catherine sat down with her lunch, wondering what was going on. From what she'd seen, everyone liked or at least respected Call-Me-Lance. She'd heard laughter from the other end of the bullpen, so they clearly didn't find their work environment oppressive. Bringing in food for everyone every week was a truly decent thing to do. Call-Me-Lance gave all the appearances of being a great boss.

What was it about her that had set him off?

She reviewed her behaviour from the first day. She'd arrived early. She'd been polite to everyone. She'd been dressed appropriately. She'd received her instructions in a professional manner.

She wasn't a perfect person, sometimes she did stupid stuff, made mistakes, said something tactless, but she was sure she hadn't done anything to earn Call-Me-Lance's disdain.

Well, sometimes people just got a bad vibe off other people.

There was nothing she could do about it but her job.

She took her full lunch hour, reading off her Kobo to give her brain desperately needed stimulation.

Then she returned to her computer for three more hours of search, click, and drag.

And, at 5:15, was gifted with another visit from Call-Me-Lance.

"Summarise some of the emails," he commanded.

She considered, for a moment, making something up, confident he would have no idea that was what she was doing, but she wasn't going to let him drive her to lies. "I am organising the emails into folders." As she had said the day before.

"You're saying you still haven't read anything."

"Yes."

He crossed his arms. "I don't tolerate slackers."

She said nothing. She had nothing to say. She had told him what she was doing and there was no reason to repeat herself.

From the way he scowled, she got the feeling he was used to people falling all over themselves to justify themselves to him, to pacify his anger. "Do you want this job?"

Yes, but not enough to grovel for it. But almost by itself, her mouth opened and she ended up repeating herself after all. "I find putting a little effort into organising -"

"That's the same excuse you've used every day. Do better tomorrow."

Catherine had to bite her lip to keep from smiling, because running through her head was, *Good night, Westley. Good work. Sleep well. I'll most likely kill you in the morning.* Except she was getting only the threats, not the compliments.

After Call-Me-Lance stalked away, Catherine looked up the lawyer's name and contact information in the file. She wrote an email.

Dear Ms. Levitt:
I am the temporary worker Create and Conquer
hired to arrange the emails for you. I'm eager for
any suggestions you might have.
Sincerely,
Catherine Aherne

If the lawyer was charging a thousand dollars an hour, and she was charging in six-minute units, as most lawyers did, that email cost C and C one hundred dollars.

Heh.

Chapter Six

"Are you coming into lunch?" Seth asked her the next day.

"No, I don't want to horn in on anyone."

"We're really a friendly group."

With each other. "Lunches like this are meant to thank everyone for their hard work. I'm not a part of that."

Seth gazed over at the other end of the bullpen. "Maybe we shouldn't have put you so far away from everyone else."

"I wouldn't be able to concentrate if I were close to them. I wouldn't get any work done."

He didn't look convinced.

To cut off further invitations, she brought out the big guns. "I shouldn't be eating pizza."

And he leapt to the stereotypical conclusion. "A slim young girl like you shouldn't be on a diet."

She wasn't on a diet. She saved all of her heavy eating for the weekend. And Friday, which everyone with sense knew was the first day of the weekend.

But he shouldn't have assumed she was on a diet. Maybe she was lactose intolerant. She wasn't, but she could have been.

Or maybe she was irritated with Seth when he didn't deserve it. The job was getting to her. "I'm feeling a little slow this morning and the energy drains out of me when I have a big meal."

"Productivity does sink like a stone on Thursday afternoons," Seth agreed.

"Yeah. I'm thinking of taking a walk to wake myself up a little." Actually, she would do that.

"All right. Know that you can change your mind."

"Thanks."

That morning, she had packed her lunch in a small cooler bag, so she wouldn't have to go to the lunchroom at all. She had made herself a ham and cheese sandwich, handy to eat while walking. She went to the concrete park beside the building and spent half an hour soaking in the sun. It was relaxing.

Then a brisk walk around a few of the city blocks. That wasn't quite so relaxing, with the crowded sidewalks, the construction, and a few psychotic cab drivers, but it was invigorating.

She was the first to return to her computer.

Search, click, drag.

The others drifted out of the lunchroom and down to the end of the bullpen, staying on the other side of the floor. There was a lot more chatting than work going on. It was loud. Maybe she should bring in her noise cancelling headphones on Thursdays.

Search, click, drag.

At 5:08, Call-Me-Lance was once more crowding her into her table. "What have you done?" he barked.

"I am almost finished the initial organisation."

He practically snarled. He bent down, and she jerked back so his face wasn't right in hers. "I've had enough," he hissed. "If you don't have anything useful to tell me by the end of the day tomorrow, I'll be telling Fast Act to terminate the contract."

It shouldn't have been a shock, and yet it was. Yes, he'd shown dissatisfaction every night, but she'd assumed he was just getting his little jollies bullying her. He had to have some understanding of the enormity of the task. And what she was doing made perfect sense. Whenever one undertook a large endeavour, one laid the groundwork first. The research for an essay. The foundation for a house. The legal documents for a business.

The threat was a cold jolt to her stomach, and she found herself trying to explain. "Sir, there are over - "

He straightened and raised a hand. "Don't give me excuses. I didn't get where I am by floating moochers. Get it done or you're gone." He walked away.

Rage replaced her fear as she glared at his back. No one had ever called her a moocher. In her life.

MacCallan crowded me, displayed aggressive
behaviour, and threatened to fire me.
Left office at approximately 5:14.

She logged out of the computer and went home. She skipped her workout and cracked open a fresh bottle of wine. It took her three glasses and an hour of watching *My Drunk Kitchen* on YouTube before she was calm enough to call Lina.

"He threatened to fire you?" Lina screeched.

"Yeah."

"That bastard!"

"Yeah."

"You're better off without that job anyway."

While Catherine was still angry, the fear had come creeping back. "I've never gotten a complaint. If MacCallan terminates the contract, Fast Act might never give me another job."

"You work with other temp agencies."

"None of them give me work as reliably as Fast Act, and word can get around. This could be a real problem." If she couldn't rely on regular temp work, she wouldn't be able to run a car. She might have to move into a bachelor apartment.

"Get in there first," Lina urged her. "Tell them how he's been treating you."

Catherine considered it. "It would be his word against mine, and his is worth more," she concluded reluctantly. "Which do you think Fast Act will care more about keeping, a client or a temp? People like me are a dime a dozen."

"So what are you going to do?"

After a few moments, Catherine said, "Skip ahead. Read some of the emails and try to put something together that looks impressive. If that gets him off my case, I can go back to doing things the proper way. I'm almost done this part anyway."

"You need to write a bestseller. Buy a castle in Scotland."

"I'll get right on that," Catherine said drily.

"Do you still want to go out tomorrow?"

"Definitely. I'll either need to drown my sorrows or celebrate." Though 'celebrate' might be too strong a word, even if she kept the job. If Call-Me-Lance was going to indulge in the habit of constantly cutting her down, the next day and five weeks were going to be a nightmare. "I've got to try to get some sleep."

"It's early."

"I'm useless for anything. I'm tired."

"Call me again if you need to. Any time."

"I will. Thanks."

She went to bed, but she barely slept, despite the wine and her fatigue. She kept running the figures in her head. She had enough to pay the following month's rent, and the bills. Amazon would pay at the end of the month, and while sales hadn't been great, they hadn't been awful, and she was due for a Smashwords payment in October. If she got a call from Fast Act the next morning telling her to never bother going to C and C again, she wouldn't be desperate. Yet. But it would prey on her.

She tried not to think about it. She couldn't help thinking about it.

Chapter Seven

Friday, September 18, 2015
Arrived approximately 6:20 am.

Catherine had assumed no one would be there that early. She'd been wrong. There were three people in their offices on the left side of the floor, and two in the other end of the bullpen. Those two surprised her by waving at her. She waved back.

The three coffee makers were already full of hot, fresh coffee. Thank god. She felt a wreck.

Her plan was to choose one of the email folders and read through the first six months, from September of 2010 to February of 2011. She would only skim them, checking for the names of the Under-Ware employees and the use of the word In-Ect, and nothing else. Once she hit the end of February, she would move to another person's folder and go back to the beginning. She would create a list of as many senders, recipients, and references to Under-Ware or In-Ect as she could, as well as some bullshit summary about whether what she had read was useful.

She hated doing things in such an inefficient manner, but if she wasn't fired, she could go back and do it properly, and if she was fired, it wouldn't matter.

She thought of starting with Call-Me-Lance's folder. It made the most sense. It was his company, and he was the one who had the close relationship with an Under-Ware employee.

But she could imagine him tearing a strip off her for wasting time by reading his emails; he knew what he'd written, he would no doubt claim. Even if what he had written was five years old. She started with the emails of the first C and C employee according to the alphabet.

More people started drifting in. Some of them even said hi to Catherine as they passed. She was a little distracted, pressed to add as many names to her list as possible. She hoped they didn't think she was being rude.

There was some interaction with Under-Ware employees in that six-month span in that folder, but no mention of any software. Nothing more than 'Hey, how're you doing,' and 'Let's go out for drinks.'

Not relevant to a lawsuit, but kinda sorta in the same universe as it, so Catherine started a new folder, giving it the name of *18/9/15*, and copied the emails into it. She moved on to the next name.

And, when nothing was there, to the next. A few more social emails from that sender. She copied them into *18/9/15*.

She was aware of Call-Me-Lance passing from time to time. Previously, he hadn't been near her workspace much, aside from his little displays of aggression at the end of the day. While her computer was relatively close to the door to reception, it was still a few metres away, and while if Call-Me-Lance were to walk straight from the door to his office he would naturally be brought by her, that wasn't his usual route. He tended to walk through the door, immediately take a right to the lunchroom for coffee or some mingling, take a right upon leaving the lunchroom to go to the far end of the bullpen to be all dudebro with his employees, and then go to his office.

Not that day. That day, at roughly hourly intervals, he found a reason to walk by behind her. Never saying anything, just there, reminding her of the sword hanging over her head.

Bastard.

Her lunch was a sandwich at her table, and coffee she had chosen to buy from the coffee shop on the main floor.

By three o'clock, she had copied over five hundred emails into her *18/9/15* folder. None of them referred to In-Ect software. All the emails sent to Under-Ware employees or referring to Under-Ware employees addressed only the arrangement of social plans. Catherine was aware that business was often discussed over drinks, but none of the emails reflected that.

That wasn't what Call-Me-Lance would want to hear, though. Catherine needed a way to make her findings seem positive without expressing a concrete opinion.

Well, she hadn't spent ten months as an articling student without learning anything.

Memo
To: Lance MacCallan, CEO
From: Catherine Aherne
Date: September 18, 2015
RE: Update on Email Assignment

Emails sent by Arthur Abrams, Jim Anand, Jeff Arnold, Tad Baker, Dev Bentall, Kevin Brown, and Spencer Chernov read, dates from September 1, 2010 to February 28, 2011. 519 made references to Under-Ware and/or employees of Under-Ware, namely Louis Doiron, Drew Marple, Leanne Gretchen, and/or Will Griffiths.

While there is no mention of software of any kind or other projects, these emails demonstrate that a great deal of interaction regularly took place between employees of Create and Conquer and Under-Ware.

She printed the memo, using the photocopier squeezed in near the basketball basket – which she had not seen anyone use – at 4:30, as she couldn't be sure when Call-Me-Lance would decide to bring down the hammer. Then she went back to doing her job the right way.

He made her wait until 5:32.

He didn't crowd her by standing right beside her chair. Instead, he crowded her by leaning against the edge of the table.

And he smiled.

Catherine's tension rose by another notch.

"Have you ever been to Hy's Steakhouse?" he asked.

His voice was lower than usual. Smoother. It creeped Catherine out. "Yes."

He seemed surprised. "Oh. I didn't think - " He stopped abruptly, perhaps aware he'd been in danger of saying something insulting, something along the lines that she surely couldn't afford an eating establishment favoured by politicians and journalists, and wasn't that a sad state of existence?

No, she couldn't go to what had been one of her favourite restaurants as often as she had as a lawyer, but she could still manage it now and again, if she accounted for it in her budget.

He couldn't have stopped himself because he was worried about insulting her. He hadn't been worried about insulting her all week.

He smiled again, a slight curl of the lips she probably would have found appealing if he hadn't been such an ass. "Why don't we go?" he said, his voice resuming that low, smooth tone. "It's usually impossible to get a reservation on a Friday this late in the day, but I can probably convince the management to make room for us." He winked.

By having someone else's reservation cancelled? Charming. "I have plans." Not used to giving such blunt refusals, she softened the rejection with a, "Sir."

He laughed. "Sir! You make me feel old. Call me Lance."

Never in a million years.

She picked up her memo. "I've put this together to demonstrate - "

"I have the feeling we got off on the wrong foot."

He had a *feeling* 'we' got off on the wrong foot? *Feeling? We?*

"I'll take you out to Hy's and we can start over."

There would be no starting over until he apologised. The apology would have to be genuine. It would have to include the words *sorry* or *I apologise* or *I was wrong*. Nothing like *I'm sorry you were offended.* And it should be in front of the same audience as had been present for his initial attack. "I have plans," she repeated.

"You can put them off," he said dismissively, under the delusion his company was worth disrespecting people she actually liked. "You've got the whole weekend. Tell them your boss is showing a special interest in you and it would be good for your career."

Creepy creepy creepy. And, technically, he wasn't her employer. Fast Act was. "I don't change plans for anything less than illness or an emergency."

He leaned a little closer, still smiling. "Come on. You can't turn me down. I'm all alone on a Friday night and that's sad."

Was that a puppy dog look he was trying to give her? "I've written a - " she began, trying to redirect the conversation down a more appropriate and less disturbing path.

"Are you really going to let me wander around downtown all by myself? Surely you aren't so heartless."

She couldn't believe he thought he could treat her like trash all week and then expect her to jump when he dangled steak in front of her.

No, she could believe it. That was the little fantasy world many obnoxious people lived in.

She had many things she could say. *Are you going to read this memo or what? Are you firing me or not? Don't call me Shirley.* But she was an incredibly wise woman and she kept that all to herself. "Excuse me, sir. If I don't head out now, I'll be late." She put the memo on the table and slid it towards him. "Have a good weekend. Sir." She turned to her computer and logged out.

"One of those who ride the five o'clock express, are you?" he asked with a sneer.

And the real Call-Me-Lance was back. She could have pointed out that a temp hired to sort emails and given the reception she'd gotten could hardly be expected to go above and beyond. She could have pointed out that it was, in fact, past five o'clock. Instead, she said, "When I come in before 6:30? Yes. Sir. Was there anything else?"

He scowled and left without another word. And without taking the memo.

Catherine stared after him. What had that bizarre one-eighty in his behaviour been about?

MacCallan crowded me and asked me out to dinner, becoming irritated and mildly insulting when turned down. Didn't take the memo I'd written demonstrating what I had done so far. Didn't tell me whether I was fired or not.

Left approximately 5:48.

Chapter Eight

"Maybe he was trying to apologise," Lina suggested.

Catherine looked up at the list of movies and their starting times, and then at her watch. She wondered if she and Lina would be able to get seats. *Space Drive Five* had gotten terrible advance reviews. She hadn't expected such huge crowds. Even the lines at the automatic ticket machines were out the door. "The words aren't difficult for a mature person to say."

"Maybe he would have said the words if you'd gone out with him."

"If that had been his intention, he would have said them immediately, especially after I turned him down the first time."

"Do you think he was asking you out on a date?"

"God, no." She had spent the entire drive home, her preparations for her evening, and the bus ride to South Keys trying to figure out Call-Me-Lance's motives. "All I can think of is that Seth had a word with him."

"Seth's the nice one, right?"

"Yeah, and he seems to be observant."

"But all the jerk had to do was back off. He didn't need to take you out to dinner."

Catherine shrugged. She didn't have an answer for that.

"I think you should have gone. Ordered the most expensive steak. And lobster. And champagne. We could have done this tomorrow."

Catherine knew Lina had the kids coming back that Saturday. Her friend would willingly arrange for a babysitter, but Catherine didn't like messing up her schedule. "I would have said I had plans no matter what I was doing. There's not enough champagne in the world to make me want to hang out with that guy."

They did end up getting seats, right by the aisle in the front row. Resigning themselves to headaches and cricks in their necks, they took out the bags of Smarties, mints, and peanuts they'd bought at Bulk Barn and smuggled into the theatre in their purses, as well as the bottles of Coke Lina had bought that morning.

The cap on Catherine's bottle wasn't firmly sealed. She took a sip of Coke and tasted rum. Lina was a good woman.

The movie was pretty bad. There were some entertaining parts, chemistry among actors who were comfortable with each other after four movies, and the odd decent quip, but the plot was pasted together from those of their first two movies, the stunts exploded past her ability to suspend her disbelief, there were too many unnamed casualties, and there was too much needless property damage.

And perhaps she wasn't fully engaged because she didn't know whether she had saved her job or not. And she was angry that after nagging her all week and forcing her to disrupt her process, Call-Me-Lance hadn't even looked at the memo. Ass.

"Well, that sucked," Lina said as they left the theatre. "I'm not going to see the next one. Spicer's?"

Catherine wasn't sure she wanted to go to a noisy, crowded bar.

On the other hand, a quiet bar might give her too much opportunity to think.

And going home meant she would spend the whole night stewing. Alcohol hadn't been able to get her to sleep on Thursday, but that was probably because she hadn't had enough of it.

"Sure." Who needed money, anyway? She called for a cab.

Upon entering the, yes, crowded and noisy bar, she saw who was waiting for them and grinned. She didn't know how early Carol Hopkinson, Dan Koyla, and Zack Kurtzman had gotten there to snag a reasonably sized table, but the number of empty bottles sprinkled among them implied it had been at least a couple of hours.

She grabbed Lina's arm. "You didn't tell them anything, did you?"

"Only that your job is a nightmare and you needed a night out. Nothing about the jerk."

"Ok. Good." She didn't want to talk about Call-Me-Lance. It would make her tense and irritable and no fun to be around. Her friends would want to give her advice when there was no good advice to be had. All she could do was grit her teeth and bear it, and get the job done.

The three at the table called out, raising their bottles in greeting. As Catherine and Lina squeezed around the table, Catherine asked, "Aren't Viola, Bernie, and Megan coming?"

"No girlfriends tonight," said Carol. "Only our group of adventurers."

Catherine smiled. The girlfriends were great, they had to be or they wouldn't last long, but sometimes it was nice to have just the Dungeons and Dragons group.

"I heard your job sucks," Zack said bluntly.

"It does and I don't want to talk about it."

"Fine. How is the new campaign coming along?"

Catherine turned from the table. "Where's the waiter?"

"Don't even. You're our Dungeon Master and you're falling down on the job. If you keep slacking off, we'll make you buy a campaign."

Her eyes widened in a horror that wasn't entirely feigned. "I am not working with some prepackaged, mass-produced, softball campaign."

"Then get a move on."

"Fine. Can I get a beer first?"

"Ask for serviettes. I know you have at least one pen on you and you can start making notes for the campaign"

Catherine rolled her eyes. And asked for serviettes.

Chapter Nine

The next day, Catherine dragged herself out of bed at 11:30. She ate three scrambled eggs and a pan of bacon. She finished off her orange juice and resisted the coffee. Its promise of energy sang to her, but her brain reminded her it was no good for a hangover. *Later, my sweet,* she pledged.

She went to the Byward Market and emptied her wallet supporting local merchants and buying organic. She usually enjoyed wandering about the stalls and looking at things she'd never buy, listening to the musicians, and eating BeaverTails, but that day she kept it quick. Before the beer and shooters had dulled her brain, she had filled three serviettes with notes for her D&D campaign, inspired, as she so often was, by events in her own life.

At home, after putting her groceries away and throwing some clothes into the washing machines in the basement, she brewed some coffee, put on a Loreena McKennitt CD, and sat down to begin crafting her campaign

She knew at least one monster her adventurers would face. Not a very threatening one, of course. A bumbling fellow with an inflated sense of importance who over-estimated his contributions to society. His vanity would be his greatest weakness.

Maybe she would have the group stumble across a mirror. When shown to the villain, he would become so entranced with himself, his mind, such as it was, would be lost forever.

No. Too Greek.

Or he would see only his flaws and would be so horrified he would flee in terror and blindly run right off a cliff.

No, too .... Well, she didn't know what, but she was sure she must have read something like it at some point in her life.

Carol's character was a thief. She could steal all of his possessions, and his followers - who'd wanted nothing more from him than his wealth - would scatter, leaving him a broken and sobbing monster.

Or she could have him trip and land face first into a bear trap.

Chapter Ten

Monday, September 21, 2015
Arrived approximately 8:18 am.

Catherine filled out her Fast Act hour report for the previous week. As she usually did, she wrote that she had worked from 9 am to 5 pm and had taken a one-hour lunch break every day. She didn't report her real hours, because no one had asked her to come in early or stay late, and she wasn't interested in getting into any hassle for claiming extra time.

She photocopied her report and put the original on the desk in Sandy's empty and unlocked office. Upon her return to her workspace, she contemplated how to proceed. Upending her method on Friday had put her behind and, logically, she should go back to her original system of organisation. On the other hand, if Call-Me-Lance really was going to demand constant updates instead of leaving her alone to do her work, it might mean her job if she didn't have easily perceived progress on a daily basis.

As far as she could tell, he hadn't looked at Friday's memo after she had left. It was on the table exactly where she'd put it. So she could do things the right way for most of the day, then read some more emails from different folders and update the original memo by five o'clock.

She nodded and resumed separating the emails according to the names of the senders.

She got an email from Sandy saying she'd received Catherine's report.

Seth wandered by with a cup of coffee. "Did you have a good weekend?"

She relaxed with relief. If Call-Me-Lance had decided to terminate the contract, he would have surely told Seth, and Seth wouldn't be wasting time talking to her.

She gave him a genuine smile. "It was wonderful." Good friends, good alcohol, taking out one's frustrations in fiction. "And you?"

"Busy, of course. It always is when you have kids." He nodded at her computer. "How's that going?"

He wasn't going to be annoying about updates, too, was he? "I'm making progress," she answered truthfully.

"It sounds like quite the job. Is six weeks going to be enough?"

"It's hard to say this early." She had no intention of requesting an extension. She had in the past, as many people wildly underestimated how long it took to do things that weren't a regular part of their operation, and she'd never gotten any complaints, but she wouldn't be doing so with C and C. Call-Me-Lance might use that against her, somehow. If she had to tack on a little extra work at the beginning or end of the day, she would, to get the job done on schedule.

"Well, let us know if you think you'll need more time. We'll want to let the lawyer know."

"Will do."

When Call-Me-Lance came in, later than he had every day the prior week, Catherine couldn't help feeling tense again. Maybe he would fire her, maybe he wouldn't. Maybe he would cut her down, maybe he would smile. The unpredictability of it made it worse.

He was wearing a suit.

Catherine loved men in suits. She thought they should have to wear suits all the time. And this was a fantastic suit. Not one of those shiny, too-tight monstrosities that made a man's head look enormous. This one was a little more old-fashioned, but tailored for Call-Me-Lance, dark blue and showing off his broad shoulders, slim torso, and long legs. His shirt was light grey and his tie was red. His shoes were black and polished.

Definitely a sharp-dressed man.

And yet, Catherine wasn't going crazy.

He had nothing on Simon, Giles, Murdoch, Jude Law's Watson, or first season Ianto.

By 3:00, she finally, finally had all of the emails separated into folders. She added to the titles of the folders the dates, derived from the emails, indicating when an employee had been hired and when they had left, if they'd left. She would start with those that had been with the company the whole five years.

But she would tackle that the next day. Purely to bulk up her *18/9/15* memo, she followed the path she had started the Friday before, and skipped from folder to folder, reading the first six months of emails, finding no references to the In-Ect software. She included the lack of results in the memo, changed the date, and printed it at 4:30.

And at 5:17, he showed up. With another smarmy smile. Full of perfect white teeth.

Yes, very pretty. I have perfect white teeth, too, the result of years of braces and a mom who had a job with amazing benefits.

"I'm meeting some potential clients at Table 27 tonight," he said in the same deep, silky voice he had used the last time he'd bugged her. "I'd like you to come along."

She didn't know what to say to that. It was an odder invitation than the other one. It was one thing to take her somewhere by himself. To get potential clients involved was weird and risky for his own business.

"Don't worry, what you're wearing is good enough to pass."

I wasn't worried, but thanks. "I have plans."

He frowned. "If you want to get ahead, you have to work at it. Do more than the bare minimum."

And if she had a proper job with a decent salary and reasonable benefits, she would be willing to sacrifice the odd night for work, but she didn't, so she wasn't. And not with him. "I have plans." Why in the world would he want her there, even if he was playing games? How would he explain her presence? Who would he say she was? Were there actually potential clients to be met? "I've prepared an updated memo if you - "

"How soon will you be ready to go?"

He couldn't be a successful entrepreneur and be that oblivious to tone, body language, words. "I have plans."

He smiled again. "Come on. You can't turn down a gourmet dinner with excellent company. And you never know where it might lead."

Her gut was screaming that she didn't want to know where it might lead. "If you'll excuse me, sir - "

"Call me Lance."

" – I have to wrap up or I'll be late."

His expression flickered from a scowl to a strained smile, and he wagged a finger at her. "I'll get you yet." He left.

Seriously creepy.

She logged off her computer and took out her notebook.

MacCallan refused renewed offer for a report on progress. Asked me to go with him to meet potential clients at an expensive restaurant. When refused, he said, "I'll get you yet."
Left at approximately 5:21.

Chapter Eleven

The next morning, Catherine arrived at her computer to find a short, narrow theatre ticket envelope tucked under the keyboard. With a sinking sensation in her stomach, she opened the envelope and pulled out one theatre ticket and a strip of white paper.

The ticket was for a performance of the *Beatrice di Tenda* at the National Arts Centre, the date of the performance the following week. Catherine whistled at the price of the ticket.

The paper was a note: *You know who has the other one. RMC*

Anxiety spiked through her. This couldn't be passed off as anything other than a date. And it didn't make sense. Despite his two previous invitations, she knew Call-Me-Lance neither liked nor respected her. He couldn't go from contempt to admiration without a significant event – a display of brilliance on her part, saving his dog, a single meaningful conversation – occurring in between.

She was early, as usual. She took the ticket and her purse back out to the reception area – where no one was waiting - and to the couches farthest from the elevator. She took out her phone and dialled Lina.

"What's up?"

"An NAC ticket," Catherine answered in a low voice. "Box seat. With a note saying I know where to get the other one."

"That's a date," Lina declared too firmly.

"I was hoping you'd tell me I was wrong."

"You, my friend, have unwittingly set yourself up as a challenge he must conquer."

Catherine groaned. "God, that's so infantile. Doesn't he have a girlfriend? He's got to have a girlfriend. Someone that rich and good-looking would have a new girlfriend within the hour of breaking up with the last one."

"Do you know anything about him other than that he's the CEO and a jerk?"

"Just that everyone thinks he's brilliant and innovative and blah blah blah. Nothing about his personal life."

"You could ask around there."

"Sure," Catherine agreed with sarcasm. "Ask his employees about his personal life. That won't make them think I'm desperate to go after him."

"So what are you going to do?"

"Give the ticket back to him, of course."

"I wish I could be there to see it. Ooh, call me back if he says he never takes no for an answer. Or that he always gets what he wants."

"You're not funny."

"I'm hilarious. Good luck."

Catherine pressed off her phone. It was ridiculous. She shouldn't have to put up with this crap. Maybe she should quit.

She'd be damned if she would lose five weeks of pay because of alpha male bullshit.

What was C and C's sexual harassment policy?

Asking would cause questions. She would have to complain about the boss everyone seemed to like asking her out for drinks or giving her an expensive theatre ticket, when in fact drinks and free tickets were the sort of thing she'd been given by the partners at the last law firm she had worked at. Little gestures like that could be common at some workplaces. If she complained about that behaviour, the response could be that this was part of the regular culture of C and C, and maybe she, as a temp, didn't understand that was the way things worked.

She left the reception area, gearing up to go to Call-Me-Lance's office, which had acquired an aura of menace, the scene of her humiliation and the lair of a jackass. But before she did, she went back to her workspace. Glancing about to make sure no one would be passing her soon, she laid out on the table the envelope, the ticket, and the note. She took a picture of them with her phone and sent it to her yahoo email account.

Call-Me-Lance was in his office, wearing his more customary casual clothing, talking on the phone.

The glass door to his glass office was open, and she had become aware that people usually walked right in. She waited outside the door until Call-Me-Lance ended his conversation, at which point she knocked.

He grinned when he saw her and waved her in. "I trust I've given you enough notice this time," he teased.

"I don't like opera." Internally, she was cringing at the inherent rudeness of her manner, but she needed to be blunt. She put the ticket on his desk.

"Now, now, have you ever listened to one?" he asked in the soft, knowing tone of the truly condescending.

No, I go around saying I don't like stuff when I don't know what the hell I'm talking about. "Recitative dialogue drives me nuts, soprano voices make me want to rip my ears off, and I hate tragedies."

He appeared shocked for a split second, then said, "But these are box seats. The experience is completely different in box seats."

"Yes, it is. You're cut off from the energy of the rest of the audience. Feeling the shared enthusiasm is half the pleasure of seeing a live performance." *Don't say 'Thanks, anyway.'* "Have a good day." And she bolted out of the office.

She felt the tension ease from her shoulders. She had done it. She'd made it clear that it wasn't about having plans, it was that she didn't want to socialise with him. He would leave her alone. He had to have more important things to do with his time.

And because she didn't have to worry about him anymore, she could fully focus on her work.

She logged on and went to the MacCallan folder. She went to the first email listed from September of 2010 and started reading.

When he said they'd given her all the emails, he'd really meant all of the emails. About half of them had nothing to do with work. Setting up dinners for this reason or that. Complaining about the snow. Calculating the Senators' chances of getting the Stanley Cup. No, she wouldn't have wanted to pay a lawyer to go through all of those, either, no matter what the hourly rate.

Then, emails only tangentially related to work. The pizza that had been brought in the week prior had been terrible and they needed to find a new restaurant. Everyone could take off early that Friday. Who was going to participate in the Fun Run?

And then, emails that Catherine was appalled she was allowed to see. She had already picked up that Seth had built C and C with Call-Me-Lance, but it appeared that there had been a third partner. As she read through Call-Me-Lance's folder at the second year mark, she saw an intense exchange of emails between him and Seth about forcing the third partner, Richard Hurd, out.

She was disappointed in Seth, the emails made him look a little ruthless, but she reminded herself that a business had to make tough choices at times, and people often came off harsher in emails than they truly were.

There was a great deal of discussion about why they were doing it. Hurd's failure to meet his responsibilities, though the emails were vague about what those responsibilities and failures entailed. Everyone hated him and he was bad for morale. And, interestingly enough, they suspected his marriage was about to hit the skids and a lawyer had advised Call-Me-Lance that the shareholders' agreement hadn't addressed the possibility of one of the shareholders getting divorced. If Hurd's wife became an ex-wife, she might gain enough shares to exert some control over the management of the company.

A shareholders' agreement with holes in it. Catherine could understand the desire to skip over all of the work, time, and expense that went into drafting proper legal documents. Everyone was excited and eager to get started, everyone liked each other and was sure they could handle any difficulties reasonably, and lawyers were soulless blood-suckers scrounging for every cent. Still, it was so damn stupid, and the consequences could be catastrophic.

Then there was the brainstorming about how to get rid of Hurd. Could he be manipulated into believing there were better opportunities elsewhere? Maybe arrange for François to give him an offer? *Who was François?* Should they bring to his attention all of his deficiencies and threaten a humiliating dismissal if he didn't leave voluntarily? *Bad idea. Could trigger a lawsuit.* Should they offer him a ludicrously high price for his shares?

What had possessed them to put all of that through emails? It appeared the emails had been between only Call-Me-Lance and Seth, and maybe they had thought that was better than face-to-face or phone contact where they might have been seen or overheard, but still, it was incredibly careless. If she could so easily be granted access to all of the emails by someone Catherine suspected was one of the IT crew instead of Call-Me-Lance or Seth, so could anyone else.

They'd probably forgotten the emails existed.

She almost resented the interruption of the story when she came across emails that had some references to the In-Ect software, which finally started around June of 2012. Vague references only, and only within the company. Proposals that there was room for another online social networking site, there was the potential to make a ton of money, and maybe they should get so-and-so to look into it. She started a new folder, *References to In-Ect Software*, and moved the emails to it.

In August of 2012, the discussion about Richard Hurd stopped, with no details about how he was convinced to leave. Catherine nipped over to Hurd's folder and looked through the emails from June to September of 2012. His emails ended in September, and they gave no indication that he was aware of Call-Me-Lance and Seth's exchanges. His final email was a mass one to everyone at C and C, announcing he was going, telling everyone they had been great to work with, and wishing them all the best. Catherine couldn't perceive any bitterness, snark, or passive-aggressive jabs in his words.

Still, just because he put on a good show didn't mean he hadn't felt resentful, and resentful people could act out of spite. If she were responsible for actually finding the person who might have stolen the ideas behind In-Ect, she'd take a closer look at him.

She went back to Call-Me-Lance's folder.

Emails about Annual General Meetings. God. That meant reading all of the attachments. She'd left boards of directors over having to read endless documents for AGMs. She knew she couldn't skip them. Development of the software might be mentioned as a goal in an officer's report. Expenses might be reflected in the financial statements.

It took all damn day to read through the AGM reports for 2010 and 2011, and none of them referred to In-Ect software. She was beginning to wonder if the five-year timeline Call-Me-Lance had given her was inaccurate and had sent her back needlessly far.

At 4:30, she updated her memo. It was no longer only a matter of having something to show Call-Me-Lance should he demand it. She thought it might be a useful start to whatever document she ultimately ended up sending to Levitt.

She gave Call-Me-Lance until 6:00 to harass her, both to see if he'd finally gotten the message and to show him that she was willing to go above the minimum when she chose to.

When he didn't appear, her spirits rose. He *had* gotten it. Or he'd become bored with the game. Or he had suddenly become too busy. She didn't care what the reason was, as long as he left her alone.

> *MacCallan gave me a ticket to a performance at the NAC. While he didn't explicitly state he expected to go with me, I would propose the note he left with the ticket, see photo, makes it reasonable to assume that was his intention. I refused and returned the ticket to him.*
> *Left approximately 6:04.*

For the first time since she'd started working at C and C, her mood stayed high as she drove through the frustrating rush hour traffic. She hadn't realised how heavily the interactions with Call-Me-Lance had been weighing on her. It had probably lowered her productivity and made the work feel worse than it might have in less annoying circumstances.

When she got home, she actually felt like exercising.

After she had showered and eaten, she got online, googling Lance MacCallan. A lot about how fabulous C and C was, and some of his appearances at various tech and software conventions, but nothing about anyone in his personal life.

He had a Facebook page, of course. It was friends only, but he had publically listed the names of his high school and university and a bunch of pages he had liked. It wouldn't be difficult to make up a fake Facebook page, claiming she'd gone to the same university and shared some of his interests. Given the number of friends he had, she guessed he didn't think too carefully about accepting friend requests. She could find out all kinds of things about him.

But no, that would be too creepy. While it would have been handy to throw the name of his girlfriend, if he had one, in his face, he would know Catherine had been looking for information about him, and she doubted his ego needed that kind of boost.

As she was already cyberstalking people, she decided to google Richard Hurd. She found nothing more than a Facebook page, friends only, and a LinkedIn account, which she couldn't access. Nothing about him starting a company of his own, or joining anyone else's.

She sat back in her chair, trying to think of where else to look.

Then she realised she was wasting her free time on C and C's behalf, when she had far more interesting things to do.

Such as rounding out the monster in her D&D campaign.

Chapter Twelve

When Catherine arrived at C and C at approximately 8:03, there was nothing unexpected at her workspace. She sighed with relief and happily logged on. But before she jumped into reading massive amounts of C and C emails, she sent a quick hello to Seth. He had been friendly and she wanted to show him that she appreciated that, but she also thought, after Call-Me-Lance's attacks on her work ethic, that it might be wise to have evidence of her actual hours. One never knew when evidence might come in handy.

Through Call-Me-Lance's emails, she saw the company go through a shaky patch when it looked like its survival might be in doubt, projects that had worked and projects that had flopped, a very long lecture about people claiming too many expenses, and employees coming and going.

Even though it wasn't part of her job, Catherine took some paper from the photocopier and started a list of employees who had left. She couldn't help being curious about the possibility that one of them had done something worth mentioning to the lawyer after they left C and C.

After June of 2012, emails about In-Ect really picked up. They increased in frequency. The AGM attachments for the later years talked about the exciting new project, how much had been spent and how much would be spent, and the potential for everyone in the company to benefit from it.

Catherine knew absolutely nothing about designing software or how people created social sites, but she had thought things needed to happen much more quickly than that, in order to take advantage of the market. If they had started in mid-2012, and it had been a viable idea, why hadn't they launched something by 2015?

In late 2012, Call-Me-Lance started exchanging emails with Patrick Dale about In-Ect. In the beginning, those emails didn't say much. References to conversations the two men must have had on the phone or face-face. Emails from Call-Me-Lance about how excited they were. Responses from Patrick agreeing that the idea had potential.

Then, a little more substance. An indication on Patrick's part that the project might be something Under-Ware could be a part of. Plans for meetings to talk about the project. Promises to send drafts of designs, suggestions for potential investors, and jokes about what they were going to do once they were billionaires.

But nothing that could be described as actual details about the software. A vague description about how In-Ect would be used by customers, but no nuts and bolts. Catherine wouldn't have been able to understand the nuts and bolts had they been included, but she would have recognised the significance of them. There were no emails sent to Under-Ware with attachments. There were no acknowledgements from Under-Ware about documents received. If documents had been sent, there was no evidence of it among Call-Me-Lance's emails. There was no confirmation of possible budgets or division of responsibilities. There was nothing she saw as solid proof that Patrick Dale or anyone else at Under-Ware had seen enough to steal anything.

In January of 2014, discussion of the In-Ect software dropped significantly. Call-Me-Lance and Patrick Dale seemed to lose enthusiasm for it. By the end of 2014, Call-Me-Lance was neither sending nor receiving emails about it, though he was still in regular communication with Patrick Dale for social interaction.

If C and C had dropped the project, there was actually no profit lost. What could they claim in damages even if Under-Ware had stolen their work?

In June of 2015, reaction to the launch of Circle Route began. The explosion of fury in Call-Me-Lance's emails made his feelings clear on that matter. He was certain Patrick Dale had stolen C and C's work.

His initial emails were directed only to Seth, who had been on holiday at the time, asking for his opinion. Then, over the following weeks, Call-Me-Lance sent emails to others within C and C, telling them to look at Circle Route and report on their thoughts. It wasn't long before the subject of the emails moved to the possibility of a lawsuit, and everyone was warned that they would be questioned about their interactions with C and C.

If Call-Me-Lance had sent emails to anyone at Under-Ware expressing his anger or legal threats, there was no reflection of it in the emails that had been provided to Catherine.

She created another folder, giving it the title *Lawsuit,* and began moving the emails into it.

At 4:30, she updated her memo and printed it out.

She decided to go back through all of Richard Hurd's emails. She'd already read some and, as he had left the company so early, he would have considerably fewer to read. She might be able to finish his emails by the end of the day, and that appealed to her sense of order, starting with a new folder first thing the next morning.

At 5:25, Call-Me-Lance destroyed her good mood by stopping at her workspace. Her heart sinking, she silently held out her memo.

He didn't take it, but he said, "That's quite the thick document you're putting together."

It was three pages.

"Everyone is very impressed with you, talking about how hard you're working. Coming in early and staying late. Of course," he smiled, "you don't have to be quite so anti-social. We do allow people to talk to each other here."

Catherine had a hard time believing the others, most of whom she hadn't exchanged a word with, had commented on or even noticed her work ethic.

"Seth thinks you're fabulous, and he's hard to impress."

Catherine found that difficult to believe, too. Seth was the only one to go out of his way to talk to her, and seemed friendly, but she had given him no reason to believe she was impressive.

"But you know," Call-Me-Lance leaned in too close, "you can't spend your whole life working. All work and no play, etcetera."

It was as recently as Monday that he had been criticising her for not demonstrating extra effort. Did he think she suffered from short-term memory loss?

"Have you ever ridden a motorcycle?" he asked.

There was absolutely no way an offer involving a motorcycle could be passed off as a normal perk of the job, or anything work-related at all.

So, a motorcycle. Was he trying to display an air of a bad boy? She had never, not even as a teenager, found bad boys appealing. They'd always seemed childish jerks to her. No doubt many would consider her boring, or old before her time, but if she wanted to hang out with grown men who hadn't matured past the age of thirteen, she would have become a therapist and gotten paid for it.

She assumed a smile. "Yes. My dad had one. Every Sunday, when the weather was warm enough, we'd go riding along the Rideau Canal. It was wonderful. Kind of peaceful. Every time I think about motorcycles, I think of my father." Probably not the image Call-Me-Lance wanted in her head when she thought of him.

He frowned. "Right. Well. Don't work too hard."

She let her smile fade when he turned away. Was he really going to do something like this every day until she left?

No, of course not. Whatever game he was playing, he would get bored with it soon. Or decide he had a company to run and that maybe he should be directing all of his attention to that.

His emails had indicated he travelled a fair amount, pursuing work and maintaining relationships with long-distance clients. She hadn't gotten any emails after September 4, so she couldn't be sure, but he had to be going somewhere soon.

She shouldn't have to put up with his crap.

But she had put up with abusive bosses in the past. She had, of course, been sexually harassed in the workplace before, though not since she was a teenager. In her social life, she'd had to endure a couple of idiots under the delusion, or who claimed to have the delusion, that to continue to apply pressure after being rejected was romantic. She shouldn't have to put up with it, but she could. After all, she only had three weeks and two days left. All she had to do was keep saying no.

Richard Hurd's emails didn't give her any substantial information. For one thing, there were very few of them. It looked like he had skipped a lot of work. He hadn't participated in any discussions involving social events organised for clients or employees. He hadn't contributed to brainstorming about any of the projects. He had been in charge of PR and hadn't been interested in anything until it was ready to be presented to the media.

Pretty much all he had done was criticise everyone else. This employee was a slacker. That one incompetent. This one ate too much of the pizza on Thursdays. That one was disrespectful. No wonder everyone had hated him.

MacCallan asked if I had ever ridden a motorcycle. While this wasn't a blatant invitation, I believe it's reasonable to assume that, given his pattern of behaviour to date, it was intended as one. When I told him I had often taken motorcycle rides with my father when I was a child, MacCallan seemed to lose interest in the subject.

She emailed a short good-bye to Seth.

Left approximately 6:37.

Chapter Thirteen

After logging on the next morning, Catherine sent a hello to Seth and decided it made sense to check his email folder next, to get the last partner done. She started in September of 2010, even though she had become confident that there wasn't much worth reading until 2012. She would regret not reading all of the emails, would worry she had missed something, and she wanted to be able to say she'd read every email, should anyone ask.

Every single frakking email.

Seth didn't send nearly as much personal email as Call-Me-Lance did, which increased Catherine's respect for him. There were references to meetings with Patrick, both socially and for work, but the emails didn't describe what was said. Seth met with clients and prospective clients. He travelled a bit.

Most of what he sent was related to finances. Pleas to hand in receipts for expenses. Warnings that people were abusing their expense accounts. Deadlines for budget projections. New deadlines for budget projections. Threats to stand right over everyone, a person at a time, while they completed their budget projections. Releasing draft financial statements before AGMs and final financial statements after AGMs, all of which Catherine had already read while going through Call-Me-Lance's email.

Seth did refer to the software project now and then, but nothing substantive.

What the unprofessional side of Catherine found far more interesting was the evidence that Call-Me-Lance was not universally adored after all. While going through Seth's emails, Catherine could see that, over the five years, a few people had complained to him about their CEO. Grievances commonly contained phrases such as 'massive ego,' 'out of control,' 'rejects opposing views,' and 'steals credit.'

Seth said he would handle things, in the emails he sent in response, but not how. The complaints hadn't been forwarded to Call-Me-Lance via email. Perhaps the issues had been addressed with Call-Me-Lance face-to-face. Perhaps Seth had brushed them off.

All of those who had complained had left the company, though if it was because of Call-Me-Lance, it wasn't reflected in the emails Catherine had. She added their names to her list of people to follow up on later, if she had the time.

At 4:30, she printed off an updated memo.

At 5:18, Call-Me-Lance stopped by her workspace.

She should have taken off at 5:01, but she liked to stop at a natural break in the work, not according to what the clock said.

Call-Me-Lance leaned against the table and gave her a smile. "Have you ever been horseback riding?"

What image was he going for that time? Cowboy? The lord of the manor? Knight?

"I took lessons in show jumping for a couple of years when I was a teenager," she said. "Then, one day, our trainer disappeared, with no warning and no explanation. The man who replaced her was rude and impatient and I pretty much hated him by the end of the lesson. It was supposed to be for fun, I wasn't training for the Olympics or anything." Call-Me-Lance opened his mouth to speak, but she kept going before he could get a word out. "I went home that night and told my mother I was never going back. She was angry and made me compensate her for the cost of the lessons from my allowance. It took over two months, but it was worth it." That was all true. "Then, a few years later, we all learned that his interest in horses was, shall we say, unnatural." That was a lie, but the way his eyes widened with horror told Catherine that Call-Me-Lance believed her. "Whenever I think of horses, my mind goes to unpleasant places."

And now it always would, damn it. She'd done it to herself. She didn't ride anymore, but whenever she saw horses on TV or in movies, she'd remember her false story and cringe.

She wondered if Call-Me-Lance would try to change her mind, try to convince her that it would be different with him.

But it seemed that she had rattled him, because he gave her a sickly smile and said, "I understand," before heading back to his office.

Catherine turned to her monitor and grinned. Then, she went to her C and C email account and composed an email.

Dear Ms. Levitt:
A reminder that I'm open to any suggestions from you regarding the organisation of the emails. Please find attached a summary of what I've done so far and let me know if there are any changes I should be making.
Sincerely,
Catherine Aherne

And that was another hundred dollars, more if the lawyer read the attachment with any thought.

MacCallan asked me if I had ever gone horseback riding. While it was not an explicit invitation, I believe it reasonable to assume it would have become one had I not given him a description of my experiences with horseback riding, which seemed to put him off the idea.

Another email to Seth, to say good-bye for the day.

Left at approximately 5:35.

Chapter Fourteen

When Catherine logged on the next day, she found an email from the lawyer in her C and C inbox.

Dear Ms. Aherne:
That seems a suitable arrangement.
Yours very truly,
Dani B. Levitt

And there was another hundred dollars.

Nothing to a company making the kind of money C and C made, but the idea of Call-Me-Lance looking through Levitt's invoices and seeing those charges was still entertaining.

Having gone through the emails of the partners, Catherine realised it was inefficient to use the alphabet for the order of searching through the folders. Obviously, she needed to shift her focus to the folders of the developers who had spent the most time working on the In-Ect software. Sometimes she couldn't believe how dense she could be.

She started with Jim Anand. She had already gone through the first six months of his emails during her mad rush on the Friday of her first week, but she had to reread them, with more care, and this waste of her time was irritating.

Nothing until June of 2012, but once she got there, she saw the most activity on the In-Ect software yet. As the months and years passed, there was a great deal of detail that Catherine didn't understand, as well as attachments. Opening the attachments, Catherine found diagrams or blue prints or whatever they were called. But those emails weren't sent to anyone at Under-Ware. The emails that were sent to Under-Ware employees, specifically, Louis Doiron and Drew Marple, were no more substantive than any of the others Catherine had seen. 'This is exciting.' 'We're working 'round the clock.' 'Things are going well.'

Then there were emails directed only to Call-Me-Lance and Seth. 'Things are not going well.' 'This is unworkable.' 'We need more money.'

Perhaps In-Ect had been a complete bust, but few had been willing to admit it.

Again, references to the In-Ect software dropped off after January 2014 and weren't resurrected until the idea of the lawsuit developed after June of 2015. Anand's responses to being told he would be questioned about his interactions with C and C made it clear he thought he was being blamed and attacked and he resented it.

Spencer Chernov had also worked on the In-Ect software, and after reading his emails, Catherine was astounded that he was still employed. He had the largest number of emails so far, by far, and the huge majority of them had nothing to do with work. She was astonished to see him spending so much time telling his kids to stop leaving their bikes in the driveway – he'd almost run over one that morning – arranging to rent camping spots, and engaging in family drama worthy of a soap opera. Those were emails she could have skipped, as the recipients weren't employees of either C and C or Under-Ware, but she got sucked in. Out of curiosity, she picked a day at random and examined the times of each email he sent. Aside from a gap of about two hours around the typical lunch time, he sent an email on an average of one every four minutes.

His contribution to the In-Ect software, at least on email, was shooting down everyone else's ideas and complaining that they didn't have enough money to do anything properly. He hadn't communicated with anyone at Under-Ware at all and had shown no reaction to the launch of Circle Route or the idea of a lawsuit.

At 4:30, she updated and printed her memo.

At 4:49, Call-Me-Lance showed up.

She held back a sigh. What was it going to be that day?

"Did you know I have a pilot's licence?"

Why would she know that?

"I have my own plane at a private airstrip. The trees are starting to turn in Gatineau Park and there's nothing like flying over them."

She had flown over them, once, in an air balloon, but flying over them in a small plane sounded even better, and if someone else were making the offer, she would have been all over it. "Flying makes me constipated."

His jaw dropped, but only for a moment, and then he snickered. "All right, all right, you got me." He glanced over to the other end of the bullpen. There weren't many employees there. "How about – Can we go to my office?"

She didn't want to, but she didn't know how to say no to something any boss might say to any employee, so she nodded and stood. It had been her intention to walk behind him, or at least beside him, but no, with a sweeping gesture of his arm he caused her to feel compelled to walk before him, him right on her heels.

She couldn't help wondering if anyone was watching her. She glanced at the bullpen. Everyone seemed absorbed in their work or their own conversations.

It was odd, but she felt more vulnerable in Call-Me-Lance's office than she did at her computer, even though her workspace was farther away from everyone else.

"Please, have a seat." He pointed at one of the chairs immediately in front of his desk while he closed the door.

She did not like it, that he closed the door.

Don't be ridiculous. Everyone can see through the walls. They would hear me if I shouted.

Call-Me-Lance sat on his side of the desk, leaning back in his chair. Choosing not to crowd her, which made her feel a little better about the situation.

"You see right through me, don't you?" he asked.

Um. She didn't know how to respond to that. Did she feel she was one of the few people who knew he was an ass? Yes. Could she say that? Obviously not.

"And you're not going to put up with any of my shit."

She'd been putting up with a lot of his shit.

"Do you know how rare that is?" He chuckled in what looked like disbelief. "I mean, yeah, I've had people call me on my crap before. Like Seth. He doesn't let me get away with much. But he's known me forever. People I've always known, they'll tell it like it is, but it seems since C and C took off," he shrugged, "no one I meet now is willing to be straight with me. They'd rather kiss my ass and squeeze every dollar out of me than tell me something they think I won't want to hear." He frowned. "And I think I might intimidate some people. I don't mean to, but it always seems to happen."

Catherine thought he might try respecting people's personal space and refraining from insulting them for no reason. In front of an audience.

Still, Catherine could see what he described happening. Someone becomes successful and others flock in to see what they can get out of it. And most of those who flocked, no, they wouldn't do anything to rock the boat, to jeopardise their own interests.

Maybe when one was a successful entrepreneur, one who was working his ass off to start something and keep it running, it was difficult to determine between those who were genuine and those who were leeches.

"But not you," he continued with another smile. "You're here to do your job. And you do it. No sucking up to anyone with the hope of turning six weeks into something more."

Huh. Had other temps done that?

"Or trying to wrangle perks from me. Or, you know, trying to wrangle *something else* from me."

Catherine didn't have any trouble believing there were people willing to go after Call-Me-Lance purely because of his money and his pretty form. Or purely because of his money. Or purely because of his pretty form.

"One found the concept of the transparent walls appealing."

Someone had wanted to have sex with him in his office while his employees were right outside?

She'd heard of stranger things. Tons of people enjoyed public or semi-public sex. Maybe a temp would feel some sense of power, screwing the boss while everyone else had to pretend they didn't know what was happening. But his office didn't seem conducive to enjoyable sex. The desk wasn't big enough to lie on, the edges were sharp enough to discourage being bent over them, the desk was too low to accommodate Call-Me-Lance's height, and the glass top would be hard on the knees. There were the walls, of course, but they would be cold, and they'd need to be cleaned up almost immediately after. There was the floor, but fluids might soak into the carpet, depending on the position. Someone could straddle Call-Me-Lance if he sat on one of the couches, which would also offer the best view to everyone else. And, of course, there was always oral sex.

Some alpha males might even go for that. A chance to show off to the underlings. *Look, everyone. This chick is so hot for me she wants me to bang her in front of you. And do you see how big my penis is?*

"She had presented … a challenge."

That could mean any number of things. Getting her to accept rejection. Getting her to accept rejection after he'd had sex with her. Employees asking when they would be getting more free porn.

"But not you. You're too professional for any of that. Level-headed. Ethical."

Yes, she was, and she didn't need to be told by the likes of him. Where was he going with all of this? Was he finally going to apologise for his behaviour?

If he was, she resented that it wouldn't be delivered in front of the same audience who had witnessed the first insult, but at that point she would take whatever she got, especially if it meant everything else stopped.

His shoulders lowered and he looked down at the top of his desk. He fiddled with a silver pen. "Have you ever heard of my father? Atticus MacCallan?"

Atticus. The first name of the person many lawyers considered their true patron saint, Sir Thomas More be damned. The inconvenient fact that Atticus Finch was fictional was ignored.

"He was a good, good man."

Was. Lance was only in his mid-thirties. That was young to lose a parent.

"Not a businessman. Not into computers at all. But strong in all the right ways. He worked hard and he played hard. He was always honest. He always kept his word." Lance smiled softly. "He loved snowmobiling. He was obsessed with it. Desperate for the first snowflake every year. Hitting the trails every weekend. Pouring every spare cent into his skidoos. It drove my mother crazy. And he took me along as often as he could. I loved it, too. Storming through the trees. Over fields. The wind and the noise and the power of the machines. It's what spawned my love for motorcycles. Skidooing in the winter, biking in the summer."

Catherine hadn't had the chance to go snowmobiling often, but she'd always enjoyed it when she had.

The smile faded from Lance's face. "Today is the one-month anniversary of his death. Cancer."

Oh, that was awful. "I'm so sorry."

He looked down at his pen again and shrugged. "I should be getting a better grip on things after all this time."

She hastened to reassure him. "No, no. A month is barely any time at all, especially when it's a parent."

"I didn't take any time off after the funeral. Looking back, I think that was a mistake. Seth could have handled things for a few days. My mother could have used the support."

That was a problem driven people had. They put their family aside because they thought their families could wait, would always be there. Then something tragic happened, and the driven people were swamped with regret.

Lance suddenly looked so tired, and he rubbed his face. "I know I haven't been handling things well. Between my father and Patrick – Do you know who Patrick is?"

Catherine nodded.

"Well, with my father, and Patrick, and the lawsuit, and we've got a product we're hoping to launch next year that's hitting some serious snags, maybe it's all too much."

Someone going through so many sources of stress, all at once, could act in very uncharacteristic ways. That could include being snippy with someone. And that's all it had been. She'd handled worse.

And he had felt badly about it, obviously. He had been trying to make it up to her. Clumsily, but that he was successful in one area of his life, in one kind of relationship, didn't mean he couldn't be awkward in others.

"So, what do you say?" He smiled; a small, uncertain smile. "I could use some cheering up. Are you sure I can't convince you to go flying with me this weekend?"

She hesitated.

To refuse to accept another attempt at reconciliation, and such a generous one at that, seemed churlish. And, given his state of grief, almost cruel. While *she* wouldn't want to spend time with a near stranger when she was feeling that awful, different people needed different things. Maybe he'd already asked everyone else he knew and, at such short notice, couldn't find anyone. She imagined Lance usually socialised with business people with families, and busy people couldn't drop everything in an instant.

Maybe it was easier for him to express his grief to a stranger, one who wouldn't be around long enough to embarrass him later, when he was more himself.

It wasn't as though she had anything that needed to be done that weekend.

And yet ….

Grieving or not, no matter what the motive, a boss taking an employee alone on such an activity felt … inappropriate. Off. And what if anyone else in the office found out? They would think she'd had sex with him. She didn't imagine they felt much respect for her, but if they thought she'd slept with the boss, they'd have even less.

And if word of it got back to Fast Act, Catherine's chances of getting further work from them would be gone.

"I'm sorry, but I can't. I already have plans."

It was the right answer, but she felt horribly guilty giving it.

"Can't you change them?" His voice was soft. "Just this once?"

And she felt even worse. She didn't have anything more pressing that weekend than groceries, laundry, and her D&D campaign. "I can't." She jumped to her feet, desperate to leave. "I'm sorry. I hope you feel better soon."

She rushed back to her workspace, but she couldn't focus on anything. Her mind and emotions kept flipping back and forth. Her choice was the correct one, but it hadn't been a kind one. What if he was genuinely desperate for company? What if he was in some sort of downward spiral?

Then you don't want to be in a plane that he's flying.

What if he really didn't have any friends or family he could reach out to? She didn't know anything about his life.

No, you don't, so why would you think you, out of everyone, could be the one to help him?

What if she came back on Monday to find he'd done something harmful? Flown drunk and killed himself? Committed a crime? Given the company away for a dollar?

Do you honestly think that's likely?

Maybe she should go back to his office and tell him she'd changed her mind.

No. When she thought of actually standing before him and agreeing, of actually being in a plane with him, everything within her screamed *Bad Idea!*

She couldn't work. She logged off and went home, where she poured herself a glass of wine and called Lina and dumped the whole conversation on her.

"It's like he's going down a checklist," her friend said.

That wasn't what Catherine had expected to hear. "What do you mean?"

"It's classic manipulation. He compliments you to make you feel exceptional. You can see him like no one else can. You'll call him on his crap when everyone else is afraid to. He manages to call you perceptive and brave while implying he's actually a modest guy. He knows he goes too far, sometimes, he just needs a strong woman like you to rein him in. And then he tells a sad story about himself to make him look vulnerable. So you'll feel sorry for him and want to take care of him and feel badly about how you've treated him in the past."

Catherine couldn't believe what she was hearing. It sounded so devious. "Are you serious?"

"Are you sure his dad is dead?"

Catherine gasped. "He wouldn't lie about that."

"Listen, I don't know him, all I've got is what you've told me, but manipulative people lie."

No. Catherine would have been able to tell. She'd figured out the tricks long ago. "Maybe we're being too hard on him. Maybe he was having a bad week and he's trying to make it up to me."

"You said yourself that you wouldn't accept anything less than an explicit apology," Lina reminded her.

"Maybe I'm being a little too rigid." Maybe Lance's father, for all his strength and honesty, had been one of those idiots who drilled into their sons the fallacy that real men didn't apologise.

"Ok," said Lina. "Let's give him the unwarranted benefit of the doubt and say he is a genuinely nice guy who happens to have the enormous character flaw of lacking the maturity to acknowledge when he's done something wrong and apologise for it."

Catherine snickered. "Way to be objective, Lina."

"Has he given you any reason to want to spend time with him? Does he make you laugh? Have you had a single serious conversation that wasn't all about him? Do you like being around him?"

"No, no, no, and no."

"Do you want to go out with him?"

"God, no."

"Then don't, and don't feel guilty about it. You're not leading him on or sending him mixed signals. And he's not a nice guy. This persistence isn't about being nice. It's sexual harassment. You know this, Catherine. I can't believe I have to remind you."

She got what Lina was saying, but after sitting there in his office, listening to him, she couldn't believe that was all fake. She couldn't believe someone would use their own father to get a woman to have sex with them.

"That bit about him going out snowmobiling with his dad," Lina continued, "sounds an awful lot like the story you told him about riding motorcycles with yours."

And that was when Catherine started finding Lina's opinion a little easier to accept. "It does, doesn't it?"

"And suddenly, you've got something in common after all."

Catherine's sympathy for Call-Me-Lance rushed out of her, and she grit her teeth.

"Catherine, you said that the partners at your last law firm told you to go with your gut. If you're dealing with someone and the red flags start going up, you pay attention. This guy has been giving you red flags from the day you started. Trust your instincts."

A detail Catherine had missed clicked into place. When Samantha had tried to justify Call-Me-Lance's behaviour that first day, she had said nothing about the death of his father. Maybe she had thought that was too personal to tell a stranger, but as far as Catherine was concerned, it was another strike against Call-Me-Lance's sob story. "I can't believe I fell for it." She felt so goddamn stupid.

"Are you going to report him?"

Catherine sighed, looking over the past two weeks, trying to recall exact words. "I don't think I'd be able to convince anyone he'd done anything wrong. If he could say he'd treated me badly and was trying to make it up to me …. He could say I'd misunderstood his intentions…. Yes, maybe he'd gone a little overboard, but it was important to him to be a good boss….Everyone else thinks he's such a great guy and he works hard to make C and C a great place to work …. And, hey, look at all these industry awards saying how awesome he is."

"I hope you're not coming up with excuses because you know reporting him will be a nightmare."

"No. I'm trying to be objective." But it was, a little bit, about the fact that reporting him would be a nightmare. Most wouldn't believe her. Those who did wouldn't want to believe her. Everyone would want to sweep it under the rug and there was an excellent chance that she would be the one to be labelled the bad guy.

"Then what are you going to do?"

"For now, my job. Maybe he'll stop now that the sob story didn't work."

"Maybe." Lina sounded dubious.

Catherine sighed again. "OK, I'm depressed. I'm going to drown myself in some fluffy fanfiction."

"All right. Call again if you need to."

"Yeah. Thanks."

Catherine turned on her laptop, but she didn't go to a fanfic site. She googled Atticus MacCallan.

It wasn't a common name, and the first link took her to an article about Atticus MacCallan getting an award recognising his exceptional volunteer work with the City of Ottawa.

On September 15, 2015.

Catherine's eyes narrowed.

She added some details to her notebook about her most recent conversation with Call-Me-Lance.

Chapter Fifteen

The next day, as Saturdays demanded, Catherine went to the Byward Market. The first thing she did was eat a BeaverTail, with Nutella, because, of course, she needed her strength.

And then she wandered through the stalls. Alluring fruit and sensible vegetables, maple syrup and, more importantly, maple sugar. Purses and jewellery she admired but wouldn't let herself buy. Sarongs that were very pretty and she would never wear anywhere. Dreamcatchers and Inuit sculptures and paintings by struggling artists.

There was a musician from Jamaica playing an instrument she didn't recognise. It looked like a large black wok with a round black lid, and he lightly tapped and stroked it, producing gentle tingly music. It was intriguing. Not intriguing enough to buy the CD, but she gave him a couple of toonies.

There was another guy with no voice worth listening to screaming classic rock. She could hear him over three blocks away. Annoying.

So was the idiot honking on the street behind her as she lingered by a stall and sniffed at various organic soaps.

Mmm. Honey and oatmeal.

Honk honk honk.

But fifteen dollars a bar. That was steep.

"Catherine!"

She turned and her shoulders slumped as she saw Call-Me-Lance in a car. He'd driven the two wheels on the right side onto the curb, and he was honking away like a moron.

"You said you had plans!" he called out.

A driver who had to slowly steer her car around him on the left gave him the finger.

His car was a very pretty red convertible. Catherine knew nothing about cars, so that was all she would be able to tell the police should she decide it needed to be keyed. "Can you drive that in the winter? I never got the point of having cars you can't drive for half the year." She could understand having motorcycles, even though their use was just as sharply hampered by Ottawa's climate. Motorcycles were fun. Cars were just cars. It wasn't as though there was a highway nearby where someone could bomb along at two hundred klicks per hour.

"I have cars for all seasons," he bragged.

"Of course you do," she muttered.

"Do you want to go for a drive?"

"No."

Her blunt refusal made him hesitate, but it didn't shut him up. "I know this little café - "

"No."

"Do you have a boyfriend?"

She was tempted to tell him that she had a girlfriend, but with her luck he was the sort of loser who thought he could 'turn' lesbians. "That's none of your business."

He grinned, wide and toothy. "That means no."

She wasn't doing this. "Say hi to your dad for me. And give him my congratulations for the volunteer award." She turned away before he could respond and practically ran into the nearest store.

She figured he was the type to leave his car there – Would he even bother paying a ticket if he got one? – and come in after her. She lingered by the front window to watch, tensing for another confrontation.

Instead, he scowled and took off, wheels squealing.

How had he come upon her? Could it have been by accident?

It couldn't have been. To see her in the crowd, her back to the street, he would have had to have been looking for her. He would have had to have known she would be in the area.

But there was no way for him to know that.

She didn't want to think about it.

Her joy in the day shattered, she mechanically worked through her shopping list, skipping everything she didn't need to look at, buying nothing she didn't absolutely have to, and speaking as little as possible.

Chapter Sixteen

You were firm, Catherine reassured herself as she took the elevator to the twenty-second floor. *You said no. You made it clear you knew he was full of shit with your comment about his father. That will be the end of it.*

There were three other C and C employees on the elevator, but they had squeezed in at the last moment and didn't know she was there, at the back. They were discussing *Space Drive Five.* They'd loved it. Anyone who bashed it was, according to them, not a true geek but a wannabe who was jumping on the geek bandwagon because it had become cool.

And then, there were just the four of them on the elevator.

"Oh," one of them – Catherine didn't know his name – said. "You're here."

Another chuckled. "Great manners, there."

The third rolled his eyes.

"I'm sorry," the first one stammered, "but you always come and go without anyone noticing. Like a ghost."

She smiled, her anxiety lightening a little. "A ghost. I can handle that."

The elevator stopped and the doors opened.

"Hi, guys!" Nancy greeted them all with a wide smile.

Nancy was always friendly and energetic. Her experience of C and C was obviously different from Catherine's. Catherine didn't know what that said about her, about Nancy, or about C and C.

Catherine and the three men returned Nancy's smile and greeting. One of the men swiped his card over the scanner and opened the door, waiting for Catherine to precede him into the bullpen. She thanked him and went straight to her workspace. She'd bought her coffee on the main floor so she wouldn't have to go into the lunchroom. Her lunch was in a cooler. She'd go back down to the main floor to use the public washrooms when she needed to.

Catherine filled out her Fast Act hour report, choosing to put down the hours she had actually worked. After the accusations of being a slacker, she was going to get every cent she was entitled to. She made a copy and put the original in Sandy's office.

She sent an email to Seth.

She started reading through the folder of another developer who had worked on the In-Ect program, Josh Guerriero.

At 10:04, Nancy burst through the door from the reception area. "Look who's a lucky woman!" she announced in a voice loud enough to be heard throughout the bullpen.

She was carrying a large crystal vase filled with two dozen red roses. No, three dozen. Catherine couldn't help smiling, because that was a sweet gesture.

The smile slid off her face when Nancy brought the flowers to her.

"Is it your birthday?" Nancy asked, still speaking too loudly.

"No," Catherine mumbled, accepting the bouquet because she didn't know what else to do.

"Well, you must have done something right this weekend," Nancy responded with a wink and a smile before returning to reception.

With shaking hands, hoping that maybe Barry had sent them for old times' sake – *He has never done that before and he doesn't know where you're working* – Catherine plucked out the small white card buried in the admittedly beautiful blossoms.

To fresh starts and new beginnings. LMC

This was beyond ridiculous.

Catherine took a picture of the flowers and the note and texted them to Lina, with !!!! as the comment.

She looked at the bouquet. She didn't know what to do with it. She didn't want it, but after the fuss Nancy had made, and with the size of it, there was no way to get rid of it discreetly. And if she did, someone would wonder why, possibly ask questions. What would she say? *I don't like flowers. I'm allergic. Your boss is sexually harassing me.*

She shoved them down the table and tried to go back to work.

Roughly an hour later, she got a text from Lina. He's upping the game by going public. Call me tonight.

Wonderful. Freaking brilliant.

Focussing on Josh Guerriero's emails was difficult. She was rattled by the flowers, looming there in the corner of her eye. And the emails were boring. Guerriero seemed to prefer offline contact, and his emails were restricted to making plans to meet.

Seth hesitated by her workspace. "Who are those from?"

"A secret admirer," Catherine responded promptly.

"With a display like that, he won't be staying secret for long. Those must have cost a fortune."

Nothing to a wealthy man.

Seth was not the only one to ask about the flowers. Throughout the day, it felt like everyone on the floor stopped by her workspace to admire the bouquet, to ask who sent it, to ask if he had been a naughty boy or if she had done something spectacular to deserve it. Between the constant interruptions and her fear that Call-Me-Lance might pounce on her at any moment, Catherine's concentration was gone and she ended up reading the same emails over and over again to make sure she understood their content.

She was tense all day, bringing on a headache. Call-Me-Lance didn't come to the office at all. She logged out at 5:01, desperate to get home.

After a supper of rum and coke and salt and vinegar chips, she called Lina. "Explain," she ordered.

"Tell me exactly what happened."

Catherine gave her the details in as a detached manner as she could manage.

"Yeah, it's definitely a stunt," said Lina. "I mean, sure, grand public gestures can be done out of pure intentions. Someone loves you so much that they're willing to make themselves vulnerable in front of others, they want the whole world to know how they feel. But it's also a way to manipulate the recipient. A guy shows up with flowers or a ring, or proposes by that thingamabob in sports arenas, and if the woman rejects him, she looks like a heartless bitch. People do that in all sorts of situations, not just sexual ones. Like someone saying in front of a group, 'Hey, I'm sure Catherine will be happy to give you a drive,' and you know that if you don't agree, everyone will think you're a jerk."

"Yeah, that's definitely happened to me." To everyone on the planet.

"Again, it's not necessarily malicious. It could be a matter of someone being a thoughtless idiot. You have to look at a person's pattern of behaviour. Whatshisname's pattern of behaviour is pretty bad. What did you do with the flowers?"

"Nothing. I left them there."

"You didn't throw them away?" Lina's voice rose into a screech.

"I couldn't do it without everyone seeing," Catherine said defensively. "I don't think you understand how huge this bouquet was and how little privacy there is in that place. But no one knows who it's from. I told everyone it's from a secret admirer."

"Yeah, but *he* is going to see your acceptance of it as a victory. He's going to think you're softening and he's on the right track. And he's going to think you owe him now because you've accepted an expensive gift from him."

"Shit."

"This will continue."

Catherine fumed silently. She wondered where Call-Me-Lance parked. She wondered if he drove that pretty little red convertible to work. A couple of her keys were quite sharp.

"You have to report him," Lina insisted.

"Nothing will happen to him. Nothing's really changed."

"Then you have to quit."

It wasn't as though she hadn't considered that a thousand times, but, "I've never left a job unfinished."

"Ah. Your pride is kicking in."

"Yeah. I guess it is."

"It's going to get worse."

"I can handle it."

Lina's sigh could be heard through the phone. "Don't accept anything else from him."

"I won't."

"Call me whenever you need me."

"I will."

"Ok."

After the phone call, Catherine ate more chips, drank more rum and coke, and watched three episodes of *Downton Abbey*.

Chapter Seventeen

On Tuesday, Catherine walked into work with a whole new attitude, having shifted from *Please leave me alone* to *Bring it on*. Let him pull his little stunts. She was going to finish the job, and she was going to finish it brilliantly. That might not mean much to everyone else, but it meant a lot to her.

That he would lose whatever game he was playing was the extra chocolate on the strawberry.

She got to C and C a little after six and looked at the flowers, mocking her with their insincerity. She glanced about, finding only the same two employees who had been in the bullpen the last time she'd come in so early, and tried to unobtrusively slip down the floor to Call-Me-Lance's office. The door was locked. While she was relieved that someone was thinking about security, it meant she couldn't put the flowers in his trash can and provide proof of her lack of interest that even he couldn't deny.

Leaving the flowers in one of the other trash cans on the floor wouldn't have the same impact, and she didn't want to talk to anyone else about them. She wanted everyone to forget about the flowers as quickly as possible. She took them down to the food court and shoved the flowers, vase and all, into one of the public trash receptacles.

She returned to her workspace, wrote the time of her arrival in her notebook, sent Seth a short email, and got to work.

Call-Me-Lance arrived shortly after seven. That morning, instead of taking an immediate right to the lunchroom, he chose to walk by her.

"Good morning, Catherine," he said in a low voice.

"Sir," she responded coolly.

His eyebrows drew together in a slight frown. "Where are the flowers?"

What an excellent opportunity he had provided her with. "I threw them out. I don't care for the person who sent them to me."

The frown smoothed away to be replaced by a smile. "I'm going to have to see what I can do about that."

He sauntered off towards the lunchroom. Catherine rolled her eyes and went back to work.

At 8:31, she received an email from Call-Me-Lance, one that had also been sent to Seth, Adam, Steve, David, and Samantha. A meeting in Call-Me-Lance's office at 9:00.

Catherine brought up the memo she had updated the previous Friday, added a little more to the summary, and printed enough copies for everyone who would be at the meeting. Then she watched Call-Me-Lance's office until someone else entered it. Seth. Steve. Samantha. Enough people that she felt comfortable joining them.

For greetings, she got an absent-minded nod from Steve, a stiff 'hello' from Samantha – Catherine wondered if the other woman still hadn't forgiven her for failing to demonstrate sufficient awe for the great boss-man – a friendly smile from Seth, and a smarmy one from Call-Me-Lance.

As before, Catherine took the seat at the end of the couch that stood at the shared walled between Call-Me-Lance's office and the one next door. It had the benefits of being the closest to the door and the farthest from Call-Me-Lance, who was sitting in the chair.

When the others had arrived and settled, Call-Me-Lance said, "Ok everyone, I've called this meeting so I can touch base with you on your projects, see what progress you've made and where you're going. I know this is last minute, so I don't expect perfect presentation."

No one expressed any annoyance or resentment, so Catherine figured this was something Call-Me-Lance had done before.

"Catherine, let's start with you."

Catherine nodded and shifted the stack of paper on her lap, prepared to hand out the copies of the memo.

"I understand you have a knack for online research."

Catherine looked him in the eye, knowing what he was referring to, but not understanding how anyone could call googling Atticus MacCallan having a knack for online research.

Though yes, she did.

"I'd like you to put aside your current assignment and do a little research for me."

Catherine scrambled to get her pen and notebook out of her purse.

"After the meeting, I'm going to send you a list of companies. For each company, I'd like you to get the names of all of the executive officers of the boards of directors, copies of their most recent annual filings and a summary of each, the products they provide, the value of the shares as of today, and any references made about those companies online in the past thirty days."

That wasn't what she'd been hired for.

"I understand that this will delay the completion of your other project, but," he smiled again, "we have no problem with you staying with us a little longer."

No. She could use the extra money, but she would be there six weeks and six weeks only.

"Thank you, Catherine."

She was to leave without reporting what she was doing. Call-Me-Lance had brought her in just to tell her of the assignment, which could have been communicated via email, in front of the others. Yes, Lina had warned her that he was 'going public,' but piling extra work on her didn't seem to fit in with his campaign of pseudo-romantic assault.

But she was happy to escape.

She closed the door behind her and looked at the stack of wasted paper in her left hand. Lina would have a fit.

About a half hour later – How much substance could there be in a meeting that length with that many participants? – Catherine received the list of companies. Twenty of them. And it was obvious she'd been given a make-work assignment. While Catherine recognised some computer software companies, which was what she'd been expecting, she doubted Call-Me-Lance gave a rat's ass what Heinz and General Motors were doing. Even if he were thinking of investing in those companies, he would have a financial advisor managing that.

Thinking about how many times Heinz and General Motors might have been mentioned in the past thirty days made her want to bang her head against the table.

He was willing to pay her to do meaningless work so he could torture her longer. Excellent priorities.

It didn't take much online searching to realise that it would take days for her to get it all done.

It would take days in the office, distracted by people coming and going and Call-Me-Lance's harassment. Perhaps not in a quiet, comfortable, safe environment.

As this wasn't why she'd been hired, and she had been given the assignment for illegitimate reasons, she wouldn't feel too bad if she skimmed the odd thing here and there. It wasn't as though anyone would read it. If she provided a document that looked substantial enough, everyone would assume she'd done a thorough job.

She googled. Using her yahoo account, she emailed link after link after link to her writing email account. It was only slightly less boring than reading emails.

Call-Me-Lance not only didn't bother her, he spent the rest of the day going to the lunchroom by his usual route along the other side of the floor.

MacCallan gave me a new assignment that wasn't part of the original agreement.
Left at approximately 5:09.

When Catherine got home, she spent half an hour in the exercise room, which invigorated her. In the shower, she indulged in stupidly expensive soap that she'd bought because it made her skin tingle. She ate a light supper of salad and grilled chicken and plugged in the coffee maker.

She resented doing work she wouldn't be paid for, but she was a writer. She was used to it. She'd pulled all-nighters before. And she had a point to make.

Chapter Eighteen

Catherine had gotten four hours of sleep, so she didn't feel too exhausted when she logged in at 8:51 and plugged in her thumb drive. She transferred to her computer the document she had created at home. She sent to Call-Me-Lance a ten page summary, attachments with all of the company documents he'd requested, and a list of every single site she'd looked at. She might not have covered absolutely everything out there, but she was actually pretty proud of what she'd put together. She'd learned a lot.

Too bad it wasn't a real assignment.

Call-Me-Lance chose not to pass by her workspace that morning. It felt like freedom.

She went back to reading Josh Guerriero's emails. As she moved into and past June of 2012, Guerriero continued his preference for offline communication. There were some emails referring to the In-Ect software sent to an Under-Ware employee, but Catherine realised Wade Anderson was an Under-Ware employee only because of his email address. His name hadn't been on the list she'd been given her first day.

The omission was annoying but not surprising. People with grand visions often skipped over the finer details. She added Wade Anderson to the people she planned to follow up on, if she had time.

Guerriero's emails stopped in August of 2013. She added his name to the list, too.

At shortly after 11:00, Call-Me-Lance and four of his employees left the lunchroom, all bearing coffee. Instead of heading towards the other end of the bullpen, they wandered to the doors to reception. Catherine assumed they were all leaving and she kept her head down, hoping to be ignored.

But no, she couldn't be that lucky. She was all too aware as Call-Me-Lance approached her workspace and stood right next to her chair.

Still, she jumped when he loudly clapped his hands and shouted, "Attention, everyone! Eyes here, please!"

She inched her chair away and looked to the side, not at him. It felt awkward, everyone would see her unnatural posture, but she was not gazing up at him adoringly.

"Seth and I have decided that tomorrow we're having lunch on the balcony!"

There were cheers from everyone.

"After all, we have to take advantage of the good weather while it lasts."

Catherine wanted to go on the balcony. Would that count as taking a gift from Call-Me-Lance?

"And, Catherine," he continued at the same high volume, "you can't keep hiding from everyone. We all get along here. I insist you join us. And everyone." He put a heavy hand on her shoulder, and she froze. "Catherine has been doing excellent work for us, including some assignments behind the scenes that you don't know about. She'll be here longer than we expected, and I want everyone to make a point of making her feel welcome."

Wow. Flashback to grade six when she transferred mid-year.

He patted her shoulder before he left.

As his four underlings drifted off, she heard one mutter, "Assignments behind the scenes, eh?"

His companion snorted in response.

Ass! Hole!

She knew what they were assuming. She knew what everyone would assume. The pathetic little temp had jumped at the chance to screw the boss. The secret admirer was no longer secret.

The others from the meeting knew what 'behind the scenes' meant, but she doubted anyone would talk to Seth about it, and she had no reason to believe Adam, Steve, David, or Samantha would care enough to dispel rumours.

Catherine didn't understand what Call-Me-Lance thought he would accomplish by smearing her reputation.

Except, possibly, protecting his own, should she file a complaint against him anywhere.

She spent the rest of the day in a fury, but she didn't let that fury stop her from working.

At 5:06, she was about to log off when she remembered she had the thumb drive with her.

All that mattered to her at that point was that she finished the job. She had no problem finishing it earlier than expected, especially as it meant thwarting Call-Me-Lance's plan to keep her longer.

She plugged in the thumb drive and transferred some folders.

Chapter Nineteen

The lure of the balcony had been too much for her. Catherine didn't care what anyone thought it meant, that she was participating. Who knew if she would ever get another chance to be on a balcony at twenty-two storeys?

But she brought her own lunch.

The balcony had wooden flooring and a steel and glass balustrade, three metres wide and seven metres long. C and C's entire staff could be out in it without feeling too crowded. The view was fantastic. It was a warm, clear day, the leaves were changing colours, and she could see parks, the gracious Parliament Buildings, and beyond them, the Ottawa River.

"It's gorgeous, isn't it?" Seth asked.

"It really is."

"Every year, we have a party here on Canada Day and New Year's Eve and watch the fireworks."

That would be amazing. An unobstructed view of the fireworks without having to deal with the crowds. "It must get awfully cold up here on New Year's Eve."

Seth shrugged. "We bundle up."

She pointed at the webbing that was stretched a metre below the balustrade. "What's that?"

"Suicide barrier."

Catherine looked at Seth with horror. "People have jumped?"

"Of course not. We had to have it built if we wanted to use the balcony. Insurance."

"Oh." And now that she knew it hadn't happened, the idea that C and C might have driven people to jumping out of the building was entertaining.

But that would never happen. C and C was a great place to work.

"Why are you eating that?" Seth flicked a finger at her ham and cheese sandwich. "I promise you, the food we've brought in is excellent."

She had no doubt it was. This was no simple spread of pizza or trays of sandwiches. This was sushi. Smoked salmon and capers. Chunks of meat on sticks including steak, chicken, pork, lamb, and honest to god venison. Portabella mushroom caps with bacon and some kind of cheese one didn't find in the regular supermarket. Little tarts filled with a grey pâté that looked revolting but that the others seemed to enjoy. Spring rolls filled with shrimp. Vegetable-like stuff Catherine had no interest in. Small bowls of broth that was apparently quite spicy. Small slices of cheesecake with raspberry sauces, tiny glasses with lime or chocolate mousse, and maple fudge. The last didn't belong with the style of everything else, but it was one of the strongest temptations. All of it overseen by a young woman wearing sharply pressed black trousers, a crisp white blouse, and a black vest with the name of the catering company on the pocket.

Catherine couldn't imagine how Call-Me-Lance had arranged something so elaborate for so many so quickly.

Well, no, she could. He had pulled strings. He had bribed someone. He had disrupted someone else's plans.

"Diet," she said succinctly.

"Discipline is all well and good, but you need to take advantage of whatever unexpected pleasures come your way. Life is too short to do otherwise."

So sometimes Seth could be a little pompous. There were worse flaws. "I've been lucky enough to be exposed to a lot of pleasures throughout my life. I can afford to pick and choose."

He shook his head. "Stubborn."

But then he left her alone. Mission accomplished.

Catherine resumed admiring the view, and she was surprised when Samantha came up beside her.

"We're lucky to have this," the other woman said.

The night before, Catherine had moved on from the folders of the In-Ect developers to those of the rest of the employees, which was how she knew Samantha, Dev Bentall, and Jolene Konishi spent a great deal of their work hours co-writing *Criminal Minds* slash fanfiction. They were quite good, and Catherine would never be able to see Reid and Hotchner in the same way again.

Did Samantha and the others know that Catherine had access to those emails? What did everyone think she was reading?

Catherine was strong enough to resist the urge to compliment Samantha on her writing and ask her if she'd ever tried creating any original work, but it was a near thing. "Yes, you are."

Samantha tsked. "*We* are," she insisted. "Lance has been singing your praises, and we're all impressed with the extra research you did. We're thinking of keeping you on longer. I'm sure there is something we could find you to do."

If Call-Me-Lance weren't such a nightmare, Catherine would have jumped at that chance. She would have been grateful for it. Instead, she said, "Hm."

"Lance is right, we have been ignoring you."

"No, not at all." Not in a way Catherine cared about. "You're all extremely busy and I'm just coming and going."

Samantha shook her head. "There's no excuse, and we feel badly about it. We all get along here. A bunch of us are going out for drinks tomorrow, after work, and we'd like you to come with us."

"Ah," Catherine stalled. She wouldn't have minded it. The slash had given her a whole new respect for Samantha. But ... would Call-Me-Lance be there?

As though reading her mind, Samantha added, "It's just a small group of us. Jolene, Dev, Kevin, Andres, and I."

The two other slash writers. She could have fun with that, either with peppering the evening with references to new perspectives she'd suddenly acquired on *Criminal Minds*, or getting them to outright talk about what they were writing.

"Please," Samantha insisted. "We're all ashamed of ourselves and we'd like to make it up to you."

Catherine smiled. "That sounds like fun. Thanks." And then, because she had to say *something*, she asked, "What's your favourite TV show?"

After a discussion about the fact that Penelope Garcia was one of the best characters in the history of TV, liking Reid better when his hair looked awful and he'd had no idea how to dress, and their disenchantment with the most recent addition to the cast, Samantha wandered away and Catherine was feeling pretty good about the day.

Of course, Call-Me-Lance couldn't have that.

"You shouldn't be eating that," he announced in a loud voice that everyone on the balcony couldn't help hearing. "We've gone to a lot of trouble to bring in some of the finest food in Ottawa. You have to try some."

Everyone was quiet, staring at them.

Jerk.

How to get him to leave her alone? "Thank you, sir."

"Sir?" someone muttered in a tone of incredulity.

"Maybe those are the kinds of assignments they engage in behind the scenes," another responded.

Low voices that didn't go unnoticed. Catherine heard a snicker.

"I'm on a diet," she added, having to unclench her teeth to do so.

"Nonsense." Call-Me-Lance put a hand on the small of her back and applied pressure. He was, Catherine believed, trying to force her to move without it being blatant to everyone watching them. "You have to appreciate generosity when it's shown to you."

She didn't have to do jack. "I need to get back to work." She strode to the door, barely remembering to step high enough to get into the building. Tripping in front of everyone would be humiliating.

Why did he have to ruin everything?

She threw out the remains of her sandwich and went back to her workspace.

She didn't want to be there. She thought about leaving, claiming she was sick. She could do her work at home. But she rarely called in sick, and never when she was anything less than a radiation bomb of contagions.

With a small sigh, she logged back onto her computer.

She hated that man.

MacCallan put his hand on the small of my back to try to force me to move.
Left approximately 6:26.

Chapter Twenty

"Are you ready to go?"

Catherine, seated at her workspace, looked up at Samantha. She wasn't in the best frame of mind for a night out. She'd just finished reading a heartbreaking series of emails that told the story of a former C and C employee sliding into mental illness.

For the first year and a half, he had seemed fine, his emails about nothing more than the projects he was working on, passing on jokes and memes, and running the lottery club. Then, anger began appearing in his tone and words. Others weren't doing their work, leaving him to carry everything alone. Others were stealing his ideas. Seth was a bully, the first complaint against the CFO that Catherine had encountered.

And then things started getting strange. He developed a fury over paying taxes. He accused a colleague of sleeping with his wife. He warned everyone that Call-Me-Lance had the whole floor bugged and was reporting everything everyone said to CSIS.

There was nothing after that.

Catherine remembered reading an email from Call-Me-Lance about Bob having to leave due to health reasons, and he hoped everyone kept Bob's medical condition in mind when they remembered his behaviour. Catherine, at the time of reading it, hadn't known exactly what it meant and hadn't given it much thought, as it had nothing to do with the In-Ect software. Looking back, she thought Call-Me-Lance's email had been discreet and showed a sensitivity she wouldn't have expected of him.

She couldn't understand it, how Call-Me-Lance could show such decency in some areas and be such an ass in others.

Catherine wanted to go home and try to forget where she worked, but she hated cancelling on people. "Give me ten minutes?"

"Ok. We'll be in reception."

Catherine had little to do to update her memo, as no one she had read that day had discussed In-Ect or Under-Ware. She transferred more folders to her thumb drive, noted the time she was leaving, and logged off.

She was a little apprehensive about stepping into reception, worried that Call-Me-Lance would be there. He had left the office several hours before and might have returned to the floor without leaving the reception area. He hadn't bothered her all day, and it made her edgy.

But no, Samantha was standing with only four other people, Call-Me-Lance nowhere in sight, and upon noticing her, Samantha said, "Great! We're all here. Catherine, I don't know if you've actually met everyone. This is Jolene - "

The one responsible for the steamiest sex scenes in the slash fic.

"Dev, Kevin, and Andres."

They all exchanged greetings as they got into the elevator.

"Where are we going?" Catherine asked.

"Sky's," Samantha answered.

Catherine had never been to Sky's, but she'd heard of it. It was a nightclub. "I'm not dressed for that." And it was reputed to be stupidly expensive.

"Don't worry." Samantha waved a hand. "The serious clubbers won't be there until ten, at the earliest, and we can move on to a bar."

Catherine had taken the bus to work that day in anticipation of some heavy drinking, but there was no way she was racking up a huge credit card charge on weak drinks with exorbitant prices. She would have to think of a way to take off early.

"Is it true you used to be a lawyer?" Samantha asked.

"Yeah." She didn't want to talk about it. Once she started, she tended to jump into a rant about it, and she didn't want to get into that in front of people she worked with or the strangers who were now getting into the elevator. "Seth told me you have New Year's Eve parties on the balcony. How hellishly cold is that?"

"We don't have the whole party on the balcony," said Dev. "It's in reception. We only go out for the fireworks. And even then, some weaklings stay inside and watch through the windows."

"Then there's the Polar Bear Club," Kevin added. "Every year before the fireworks start, Lance strips down to his boxers and stands out there and challenges everyone else to go out with him in their underwear."

That was a sexual harassment claim waiting to happen.

"Anyone who stays out as long as he does gets $500."

Catherine was aware that if Call-Me-Lance weren't involved, even she would almost think it kind of cool. "Anyone ever get frostbite?"

"They aren't stupid about it," Dev answered. "They check the temperature and any wind chill warnings. Last year, it was only two minutes. The longest was half an hour, but that was a very warm year. Relatively speaking."

"Have any of you won the challenge?"

"Me." Samantha smirked. "Every year."

"You're a stronger person than I." Just thinking about it made Catherine's skin pebble.

Despite all of the signs that, no, Call-Me-Lance wasn't joining them, it wasn't until they left the building without an appearance from him that Catherine was finally able to relax.

Sky's was on Sussex Street, only a few blocks away, but Samantha insisted they take two cabs, and insisted on paying the fare herself. The nightclub was just opening when they got there, and the staff seemed annoyed to have anyone showing up so early. There were plenty of booths available, along the walls, and they picked one near the back. Catherine managed to snag a space at the end, where she could give herself more room. A waitress in fashionable black clothing Catherine could no longer afford arrived and handed out menus.

Catherine hoped she was hiding her dismay as she looked at the prices. There wasn't a single drink under $15, except for the soft drinks, which were $10.

"You have to get the Hawaiian," Samantha told her. "You'll love it."

Their nascent friendship too fragile to jeopardise with outright contradiction, Catherine kissed good-bye $18, plus HST, plus tip.

She hadn't eaten KD since law school, but she could manage it for the next little while.

Mm, neon orange.

The pumping dance music had started blaring by the time the waitress returned, and they had to shout their orders at her. Samantha also asked for five different appetizers, each with a price that made Catherine want to walk out in disgust, they were so insultingly high.

Maybe she just wouldn't eat at all for the next few days.

"Do you have plans for the weekend?" she asked Dev. She had to shout into his ear.

"My family is closing up the cottage."

She saw, rather than heard, him sigh. "Are you dreading it because it's such a big job or because it means that winter is coming?"

"No, I'm just going to miss going there. We've been so busy this summer that we've only been able to get there three times."

"Where is it?"

And he was off, an ode to a cottage that was more like a house, and an incredibly nice one at that, wooden floors and a large fireplace and a hot tub. Accessible only by boat and right on the lake. The call of the loons early in the morning. Swimming, no matter how cold. Waterskiing, hiking, bonfires, BBQs, and, of course, a lot of alcohol.

The drinks had been delivered during Dev's rhapsody, and Catherine reached for hers to take her first sip and see if the Hawaiian really was that fantastic.

A figured appeared beside her, and at first Catherine thought it was the waitress. But no, it was Call-Me-Lance, crowding into the booth beside her without any kind of request for permission to do so. She tried to keep from shifting, tried to keep him out, but he was heavier than her and pushed her over with a wiggle.

Had Samantha lied to her? Why would she do that?

"Hi, everyone!" Call-Me-Lance shouted with a grin. "Drinks are on me!"

Everyone cheered.

Then he put his arm around Catherine's shoulders!

Catherine drained her Hawaiian in seconds, barely tasting it. "I have to go." She firmly set the glass down.

"We just got here!" Samantha protested.

"I'm driving. I shouldn't have more than one." She tried to calculate the cost of the drink, the tax, and the tip, but she was too rattled to do so, so she put $25 on the table and hoped it was somewhere in the ball park.

Ignoring Samantha's objections, Catherine said to Call-Me-Lance, "Let me out."

He smiled. "No."

She wondered how much it would hurt him if she slammed her high heel into the top of his foot. Maybe it would break bones. "Please move, sir."

"Make me."

God, it was like dealing with a bratty eight-year-old.

She wasn't dressed for it, it was awkward, and she had to violate Dev's personal space to do it, but she pulled her legs out from under the table and used the table for leverage to get to her feet. Heels on cushions were not conducive to good balance. Anxious that it wouldn't take her weight, she stepped onto the table. It wobbled, but it didn't collapse or tip over.

"Catherine!" Samantha chided. "You look ridiculous!"

Catherine did not care what the wait staff, the only other people there, might think of her. She wouldn't be going to Sky's ever again. Call-Me-Lance had nixed any possibility of the nightclub becoming appealing to her.

Two careful steps brought her to the edge of the table. Her dismount wasn't elegant, she basically sat on the edge of the table and slid off to the floor, but it was accomplished and that was all that mattered.

She thought she saw Call-Me-Lance reach out to grab her, but she moved too fast for him.

If anyone said anything as she stormed out of the club, she didn't hear it.

Had Call-Me-Lance asked Samantha to arrange the night out? He had to have. How else would he have known where they would be? What had he told Samantha? That he was trying to get Catherine to like him and he thought tricking her into spending time with him was the way to do it? And what had Samantha thought of it? That Call-Me-Lance was such a nice guy and Catherine was nothing but a big ol' meanie?

Three more weeks.

Or, if she could get enough done on her own time, possibly two. It was galling, the idea of working so many hours without compensation, but the fact was that Fast Act would never try to collect on unauthorised work done at home, and it might be to her benefit to avoid creating a history in which she made unusual demands.

Her primary goal was finishing the job – brilliantly – and getting out. It meant getting away from *him*. And it meant he would fail in his game all the earlier.

Chapter Twenty-One

The next day, Catherine woke just before eleven after a bad night of poor sleep. It had taken her hours to calm down enough to get into bed, and fury had followed her into her dreams. She had a headache from grinding her teeth.

She lay in bed for a while, thinking about what she had to do and not wanting to do any of it. Organise the piles of paperwork that had been accumulating all over her apartment. Dig out the vacuum. Get some cash and groceries.

She didn't want to go to the Byward Market. What if Call-Me-Lance showed up?

She could get her groceries somewhere else, of course, but she didn't want to leave her apartment at all. She didn't want to deal with anyone, not even on the superficial level of saying hi to a cashier. And it was safe in her apartment. She could control who got into it.

She crawled out of bed, pulled on jeans and a Queen's sweatshirt, and went to her tiny galley kitchen. After starting the coffee maker, she stood in front of the fridge with the door open, like her mother had always told her not to. She probably had enough bread to get through the week, if she brought some frozen dinners in for lunch. Though that meant going into the lunchroom to nuke them, and she hated the thought of that. Very few fruits and vegetables, but she could last a week on a heavier diet. Cheese. Did she have crackers? Yes, she did. She had some spaghetti sauce and pasta. Rice.

She could get by. Realising she didn't have to go out after all, her dread dissipated.

What should she do instead?

Work on the D&D campaign. Starting with eliminating the monster. Call-Me-Lance didn't deserve to be in her campaign, not even as an incompetent villain.

She had just poured herself her first cup of coffee when her landline emitted the distinctive ring of someone seeking entrance into the building.

She wasn't expecting anyone or anything.

Probably someone who had pushed the wrong number. Or who didn't have the right to be in the building and was hoping a random tenant would be careless enough to let a stranger in.

Catherine wasn't careless. She picked up the phone. "Hello."

"It's me."

A chill swept through her. Call-Me-Lance. What the hell was he doing at her apartment building?

She wasn't going to let him know she could recognise his voice from two short words. "Who is this, please?"

"That's very cute."

"I don't let strangers into the building."

"It's Lance!"

He sounded annoyed. Good. "What do you want?"

"Let me up."

"No."

"This is ridiculous. Let me up."

"No." If she had believed in a god, she would have been praying to it that no other resident or legitimate guest showed up and helpfully let Call-Me-Lance in.

"I have a surprise for you."

There was a sing-song quality to his words. Was it her imagination, or had he intended to sound menacing? "I hate surprises. Go away." She hung up.

The phone immediately rang again. She let it ring. And ring. And ring.

The annoyance of it drove her to answering. "Go away."

"It's a nice surprise."

"I doubt it. Go away." She hung up.

It rang again. And again. And again.

She picked it up. "Go away." She hung up.

It rang again.

She could unplug the phone, but in time someone would come and let him in, and he would then be pounding on the door. She had to get rid of him. She picked up the phone. "Do I have to call the police?"

He laughed, unconcerned. "I'm going to keep calling until you see my surprise."

She could call the police, and the rich handsome man could tell them anything. Maybe that he and his girlfriend had had a fight and she was refusing to see him to punish him. The police would believe him and they would think she was a hysterical drama queen with an inclination for abusing emergency services.

She could call one of the superintendents, evicting unwanted guests was part of their job, but they were all on the older side, and physically ejecting someone of Call-Me-Lance's size might be beyond them.

And with her luck, he was the close personal friend of someone high in the company that owned the building, and could get the superintendent fired as a favour.

"Just a second," she said, and she hung up. She shoved her bare feet into a pair of sneakers and left her apartment, locking it behind her. She ran down four floors of stairs because she was too agitated to wait for the elevator.

Call-Me-Lance was standing at the intercom, glaring at it. Was he trying to call her again?

His focus on the intercom allowed her to reach the door unnoticed. While he did turn towards her as she opened the door, she was able to slip through and close the door behind her before he could reach her, locking them both out. "Showing up at my home uninvited and refusing to leave is a crime."

He laughed again. "I'm taking you on a picnic." With a sweep of his arm, he directed her attention to his pretty little red convertible in the curving driveway in front of the building.

She didn't understand him. How many different ways did she have to say no? He had to be too busy to be wasting his time like this. And it wasn't as though she were some raving beauty. "I'm not going anywhere with you."

"Your attempts to play hard to get are a little weak, Cat."

No one called her Cat. Ever.

"You came out for drinks last night," he said.

"Samantha said you wouldn't be there."

"That's not what she told me."

What had Samantha told him? Had she told him anything? Was she part of his twisted game or was he lying? Catherine's brain felt like it was skittering into too many directions, trying to figure out which possibility made the most sense.

"Don't think I haven't noticed the way you keep showing up so early and staying so late, hoping to get some time alone with me."

Catherine's mouth dropped open in astonishment. He couldn't possibly believe that was her motive.

"Watching me all the time."

So she could avoid him.

"Strutting around in those short skirts and high heels."

Her skirts were no shorter than common office wear allowed, nor were her heels particularly high. And even if she were dressing to attract someone's attention, "There are over forty people on that floor. It's arrogant of you to assume I'm trying to appeal to you."

He snickered, as though the idea that she was interested in anyone other than him was ludicrous. "You can stop your little prude act."

First, she was dressing in a sexually provocative manner, then she was acting like a prude. Shouldn't a successful entrepreneur have a better grasp on internal consistency?

"Everyone already thinks we're sleeping together," he added.

"Because that's what you told them," she pointed out resentfully.

He widened his eyes with feigned innocence. "When did I ever say anything like that?"

She snorted.

"So why don't you - " He stepped closer, and she stepped back. " – come with me -" Another step forward, another step back. " – and let me show you a good time, hm?"

Her back hit the door. She angled her face away to avoid the hand he'd lifted to touch her cheek. "I am never having sex with you." There. No denying the meaning of her words that time.

He smirked. "No one who's ever said that to me has stuck to it."

He had done this to other people.

For the first time, she was genuinely scared of him.

She'd be happy for another guest or resident to show up. Any time now. It was Saturday afternoon. Where the hell was everyone?

She raised her hands to shove Call-Me-Lance away, but stopped before making contact. If she pushed him, and they ended up in some kind of he-said-she-said situation later, he'd be able to claim that she assaulted him.

She stepped to the side to get around him, reaching for the intercom, but he grabbed her bicep and squeezed.

"Let go of me!" she shouted.

"Calm down and come along." He tried to drag her towards the car.

He was begging for a knee to the groin, but her stance made that impossible. He was one step ahead of her, and she needed both feet planted on the ground to resist his attempt to drag her after him.

Most of what Catherine had learned in the karate lessons she'd taken in her late teens had long since faded from her mind, but one of the few moves she remembered involved escaping that particular hold by twisting her arm to apply pressure to the attacker's thumb, a weak part of the grip.

She'd never had to do it before. Would it work? She had to try. She twisted her arm.

He immediately released her with a hiss, standing back and holding his thumb.

Then he glared at her. "Bitch."

"This entrance is under surveillance." She pointed at the camera in the corner of the overhang. "And the superintendents are on duty twenty-four seven. All I have to do is hit the red button under the intercom."

His face flushed with anger. "This isn't over," he spat. "Cock-teases get what they deserve." He stormed to his car.

Did he usually jerk the gear shift that abruptly when he drove? It didn't seem the proper way to treat what she assumed was a fine automobile.

Catherine's hands were shaking so hard she fumbled her keys, dropping them once before she could insert them into the lock. She didn't let the door sway closed behind her on its own but pulled it shut. Her heart was racing, her breathing short and fast, her knees trembling, as she took what felt like an interminable elevator ride up to her floor. Getting into her apartment and locking the door no longer made her feel safe. She wanted to pile furniture in front of it.

How hard was it to get a gun in Canada, anyway? Hunting rifles weren't as handy as side arms but they sure looked scarier.

Don't get crazy.

She grabbed her phone and pressed Lina's number. "Please pick up, please pick up, please pick up."

Her incredibly busy friend answered. "Hi there."

"He came here!"

After a gasp, Lina asked, "He was in your apartment?"

"No, I didn't let him get through the main door. But he kept ringing and ringing and he said he wouldn't stop until I let him up, so I went down to make him leave. He said he was going to take me on a picnic. Those words. Not that he wanted to, but that he was going to." Her voice broke into a sob. "When I said no, he accused me of leading him on and said since everyone in the office already thinks we're sleeping together, I might as well do it. He grabbed my arm!"

"Call the police," was Lina's swift response.

"And tell them what? That my gorgeous rich boss wanted to take me on a picnic? Who's going to take that seriously? They'll write me off as a feminazi looking for a reason to be offended." She pressed her fingers to her closed eyes, trying to force back the tears. "He came to my *home!*"

"Do you want me to come over? I can pick up some beer on the way and we can have a *Firefly* marathon."

Lina's tone had shifted from anger to almost casual. *Let's hang out.* Calming.

Catherine wanted her to come. "Don't you have a million things to do?" With her job and school and family, Lina couldn't usually drop everything at the last minute.

"Nothing that can't wait. Do you want me to come over?"

"Yes," Catherine said in a small voice. "Please."

"Give me thirty."

Putting aside the phone, Catherine looked at her front door for a few moments. She dragged the heavy, hideous armchair she'd gotten from her brother-in-law's aunt in front of it.

Then she took a shower. A long, hot shower, scrubbing at her skin.

Chapter Twenty-Two

Lina didn't arrive in thirty minutes, it was closer to ninety, but Catherine, despite the intensity of the fear she'd whipped herself into during the wait, forgave her friend as soon as she opened the door. Lina was weighed down with not only twelve bottles of Heineken, but seven cloth grocery bags. "How did you carry all of that here?"

"I was a packhorse in a former life. Help me with this stuff."

Catherine put two bottles of beer in the freezer and the rest in the fridge, and Lina's bounty was dumped on the coffee table. Tons of chocolate, from Laura Secord to Smarties to slabs of milk, dark, and white chocolate bark from the Bulk Barn. Chips and Cheezies and dip and salsa. Black jellybeans, because the black ones were the only ones Catherine liked. A red velvet cake, some of the icing smushed in transit. Doughnuts. A tub of Häagen-Dazs caramel cone explosion and black cherry amaretto gelato. Bottles of Coke – Coke had reduced the size of the bottles, the miserly bastards – and Canada Dry ginger ale.

Catherine frowned as she picked up an enormous tray of pre-washed and pre-cut vegetables. "What the hell is this?"

"I know, I know," Lina said apologetically. "I had a moment of madness when I thought we might want something healthy amidst this mountain of crap. Don't worry, I got more than enough dip to counteract any nutritional content the veggies might have."

"How much did all this cost?"

"I don't remember."

Catherine looked through the bags and found no receipts. She glared at Lina.

Lina shrugged. "Don't worry about it."

Catherine was in no state to be stubborn. She gave up and went to the kitchen for mixing bowls. Only barbarians ate chips from the bag.

Once the beers were frosty, Catherine and Lina settled in front of the TV and Catherine popped the first *Firefly* DVD into the player. They sang along with the theme music.

"Take my love, take my land, take me where I cannot stand. I don't care, I'm still free. You can't take the sky from me."

2:45 pm
"What happened to Adam Baldwin, anyway? He seemed decent enough when the show was running."
"Abducted by aliens."

3:37 pm
"It's all about the suit, isn't it?"
"The suit. The formality and intelligence with the sarcastic edge. The dark side with the willingness to break all the rules for a loved one who is not a romantic partner. What's not to like?"
"He can't fight worth a damn."
"That's what Zoe is for."
"I love Zoe."
"Zoe's awesome."

5:54 pm.
"I'm sick of beer. Do you have anything else?"
"No. I didn't get out today."
"Dial-A-Bottle it is."
"I don't have a lot of money to throw around, and neither do you."
"I think I'm getting that grant."
"That's not for alcohol."
"Have you forgotten school? Speak now or forever hold your peace."
"Fine. Gin."
"Bombay it is."
"Not Bombay! Get the cheap stuff. I'm going to mix it with ginger ale."
"That's so disgusting."
"It's refreshing."
"You can get the St. Hubert's."

"Chicken and rib combo?"

"Of course."

"You know we won't be able to eat like this when we're thirty."

"I'll worry about that next year."

6:50 pm

"Do you think we should go on a mud run?"

"No."

7:32 pm

"See, that's how a one-episode romance should work. None of that love-at-first-sight crap."

"With the regular character having a personality transplant and turning into a love-struck dork."

"Willing to lie to everyone who trusts and respects them."

"And leave the friends, family, and colleagues they swore they would die for."

"And once the romantic partner leaves, they're never mentioned again."

"Single-episode romances should be banned."

"Unless everyone else laughs at them and the couple want to kill each other in the end."

"Yeah, that's ok."

9:10 pm

"As fabulous as Simon and Zoe are, I'm ready to take a break from them. Hey, *Princess Bride!*"

"Change the channel."

"It's a classic!"

"It's a classic I've seen a billion times. Along with a kajillion parodies. If I hear 'As you wish' one more time, I'm going to hit someone."

"You're dead to me."

"And my final request is that you change the channel."

"As you wish…. Ow."

11:22 pm

"What about climbing Mount Kilimanjaro?"

"I think that costs tens of thousands of dollars. And a lot of people die."

"Oh."

1:14 am

"That wasn't Alan Rickman."

"Yes, it was."

"No, it wasn't."

"Yes, it was."

"I'll bet you a twenty it wasn't."

"I don't have a twenty."

"You don't have twenty dollars?"

"Not after tipping the delivery girl. I think I've got a five and some change."

"Then I'll bet you a five."

"Fine. We'll watch the credits."

"This movie is crap. Which is further proof Alan Rickman isn't in it. I'm not slogging through it to the credits. Check imdb."

"Fine....Damn."

"Told you. Is it an old five or a plastic one?"

"You're really going to take my last five dollars?"

"I'm a cold-hearted bitch. Ooh, it's an old one. Do you have a black pen?"

"Of course. Why?"

"I'm going to Spock Sir Wilfred Laurier."

"Do Snape. It's more fitting."

"Oh, right."

2:09 am

"That's so not what happened."

"Yes, it was!"

"You fell off the chair before you got to the end of the song."

"I did not!"

"Yes, you did."

"You weren't even there!"

"Yes, I was."

"You left before midnight!"

"I did. For a beer run to Hull. Then I came back."

".... You did?"

"I did."

"Are you sure?"

"Quite sure."

"Why don't I remember that?"

"Because you were plastered. And you'd have to be to try to sing *My Heart Will Go On*."

"Shut up."

2:48 am

"I can't believe she didn't come to the funeral."

"You always said she and your grandmother hated each other."

"So? It's family."

"And that everyone took your grandmother's side."

"My grandmother was the sweetest, most generous woman who ever lived, and Celia was an ungrateful bitch."

"I think you've got your answer."

"It's family. She owed us."

"…."

"I hate it when you do that. Everyone knows you're judging us when you don't say anything."

"All it means is that I have nothing to say."

"Yeah, right."

"If you want to start a fight, I'm going to bed."

"I'm not starting a fight. I'm telling the truth."

"Truth can just as easily start hostilities as lies."

"Please tell me you're quoting someone and you didn't make that up yourself, because that sounds pretentious."

"I'm going to bed."

"No, sorry. I'm not starting anything. Watch TV. Drink more gin."

3:12 am.

"I'm going to vote for the Green Party this time."

"That's a waste of a ballot."

"Do you know how many pipe leaks and train derailments there have been in 2015 alone?"

"The Green Party has no chance of winning."

"Not if no one votes for them."

"We have to be realistic. The only way to get Harper out is by voting strategically."

"So you're not voting NDP?"

"Not this time. Besides, the NDP took a swerve off the path when Jack died."

"Five parties and there's no one decent to vote for."

"Aren't there six?"

"What's the sixth one?"

"I don't know. I just think I've read somewhere that there's another one. Only a couple of seats."

"Look it up."

"I'm not *that* interested."

3:33 am

"Oh, please, you were just as hooked on *Degrassi High* as the rest of us."

3:59 am

"Seriously, you have to get some better furniture. This is some seriously ugly shit."

"You said 'seriously' twice."

"I'm not one of your books. Stop editing me."

4:26 am

"What about the Tamarack Ottawa races?"

"Why are you so determined that we do something physically painful?"

"It's part of being a well-rounded person. Come on. It's only ten klicks."

"I'll do the two klick version."

"The five."

"All right."

"Great!"

"Maybe."

4:48 am

"I miss the days when CBC started the TV broadcasting day with *O Canada*."

"Why?"

"Because it was so fantastic."

"Uh, love my country and all, but I wouldn't call the national anthem objectively stirring."

"You've never seen it? It's gorgeous. It starts with an aboriginal drum beat and slowly merges into the melody, and they show the most spectacular images with it. It's majestic."

"I don't remember seeing that."

"You would remember if you had. YouTube. Right now."

"Wow."

"See?"

"That should be the only version allowed by law. They should have to show that whole thing at the Olympics."

"Great way to start the day, eh?"

Chapter Twenty-Three

Lina came out of the washroom looking as ragged as Catherine felt. "I smell bacon."

"Not from this apartment, you don't," Catherine said from her couch, her laptop balanced on her thighs.

"Coffee?" Lina asked hopefully.

"Coffee is banned. Bad for hangovers. You can have orange juice or water." Catherine remembered she hadn't gone shopping the day before and corrected herself. "You can have water."

Lina made a face at that and went into the kitchen. Catherine heard her pour water from the filtered jug and take something out of the fridge. She returned with the untouched tray of vegetables. "Maybe these were a good idea, after all."

Catherine looked at the sliced carrots, celery, cucumber, broccoli, and cauliflower. Her stomach didn't rejoice at the sight. "I'd rather have the red velvet cake."

Lina's eyes lit up. "Ooh, good idea." She went back to the kitchen and brought out the remains of the cake and two forks.

Sumptuous, revitalizing sugar.

"How do you feel?" Lina asked.

"Better. Thanks for coming."

"What are you going to do?"

"I'm not sure, yet. I'm going to talk to a few people, see what my options are."

"But you are going to do something," Lina pressed.

"I think I have to. He came here, for Christ's sake. And something he said makes me suspect he's done the same thing to other people. Maybe even worse." She'd always found it easier to stand up for other people's rights than her own.

Lina scowled. "Scumbag." She stabbed her fork into the cake.

"Yeah."

After Lina had showered and left, Catherine sat on her couch, silently contemplating her next steps.

She sent an email to a friend, asking if they could meet for lunch the following week.

Although it had always been her habit to include in her work diary only events connected to the workplace, she added information about the drinks at Sky's and Call-Me-Lance's 'offer' of a picnic. She went back to the entry of the Friday before and squeezed beneath it a description of her encounter with Call-Me-Lance in the Byward Market, making it clear that the entry had been added a week after the event.

She scanned the diary into her computer, right from the beginning, a page at a time. She printed out the scans and the photos of the NAC ticket and the roses. She put all of it into a binder with her copies of the Fast Act paperwork, the non-disclosure agreement, and her hour reports. Then she went back to the computer and printed the article about Atticus MacCallan getting the volunteer award, and put that in the binder, too.

After she put the binder on a shelf, she started reading C and C emails. Because one way or another, she was not putting up with another three weeks of this shit.

Chapter Twenty-Four

Monday, October 5, 2015
Arrived approximately 8:44 am.

Dear Ms. Levitt:
Please find attached my preliminary draft. I have
provided a summary of my findings, an index,
and all of the relevant emails I have read to date.
While I still have more emails to read, I believe
that what I have provided represents an accurate
picture of the entirety of events as they pertain
to communication between Create and Conquer
and Under-Ware.

As far as Catherine was concerned, if all C and C had were
those emails, they had nothing.

I know you are extremely busy, but I have to ask
that you give this a quick glance as soon as
possible and let me know of any changes you
feel need to be made. This Friday, October 9,
2015, is my last day at Create and Conquer, and
I'd like to make any corrections to the
organisation of my report by then.
Sincerely,
Catherine Aherne

Catherine took a deep breath as she hit send. There. She had
committed herself to being done by the end of the week. Two weeks
early.

She hoped Levitt didn't tell anyone at C and C about it. Catherine wanted it to be … a surprise.

She filled out her report for Fast Act. While she didn't write down the hours she had worked at home, she did accurately reflect her hours in the office, which had been considerably longer than nine to five, her lunch hours shortened or skipped altogether.

Of course, she wouldn't be coming in early or staying late anymore, not if Call-Me-Lance was going to claim she was doing so only to seduce him.

Ass.

After delivering the original Fast Act report to Sandy, Catherine returned to her workspace to find an email from Call-Me-Lance.

My office. Now.

Hell. Levitt had told him.

She printed the most current version of the *18/9/15* memo.

She didn't want to go to Call-Me-Lance's office. Did not want to. She hadn't felt this kind of dread since finishing her articles, where she'd dealt with the most vicious lawyers in her career, and even then, she'd never been physically afraid of being in the same room as them.

But the walls of his office were transparent glass. Surely he wouldn't try to hurt her where everyone could see.

And she would be damned if she would let him know she was afraid of him.

She squared her shoulders and strode to his office in the most blatant display of nonchalance she could muster.

And was able to see through the glass that he was working out. He was stretched out on his bench, pressing what looked like a lot of weight. He was wearing shorts and nothing else.

Catherine rolled her eyes. It was hard to be quite so afraid of him when he acted like such an idiot.

Yes, yes. Nice biceps, legs, chest, abs, waist, blah blah blah, but while she had frequently enjoyed observing a fine physique in a tasteful bathing suit, guys grunting in a gym had never been a turn on.

She was tempted to turn back around, letting him know via email that she would come again when he was fit for visitors, but she wanted to know whether Levitt had told him she was leaving. She knocked on the door.

He kept on pumping.

If he hadn't ordered her to his office, she might have believed that he was so focused on what he was doing that he didn't know she was there.

She didn't want to watch him and have him think she was drooling over his body. On the other hand, she didn't want him thinking she was afraid to look at him. She thought frowning down at her watch sent a good message, expressing impatience over the waste of her time.

Over two minutes ticked by.

He finally put the bar in the rack and rose from the bench. "Come in, Cat."

Overfamiliar bastard.

She opened the door. She was still afraid of him, no matter how ridiculous he was. He could easily hurt her. "My name is Catherine," she said.

He didn't sit at his desk, but remained standing by his exercise bench. He didn't put on a shirt, or even sling a towel around his neck. She wondered where he showered. Was there an executive washroom hidden away somewhere?

She looked him in the eye, to show him she wouldn't cower before him.

He, of course, chose to interpret that differently. "Are you shy?" he teased, gesturing down in a way meant to encourage her to look at his body.

She didn't. "I'm a Johnny Depp fan."

He tsked. "You should try to broaden your horizons."

"I broaden them all the time. In the directions I chose. Is there a reason you called me here?"

"Just to see you smile. You have such a pretty smile, but I haven't seen it often enough."

So they were to pretend Saturday hadn't happened.

"Come on, give us a smile."

"I'll get back to work."

He laughed as she turned and left. "You shouldn't be so afraid to go after the things you want, Cat."

Catherine was no expert, but she couldn't help wondering if Call-Me-Lance had a serious mental health problem. Like a narcissistic personality disorder or something. They did say a lot of successful people were psychotic.

At least it appeared that he hadn't gotten word from Levitt about Catherine's plans.

She didn't go back to work. She went to Seth's office, which was in the other far corner of the floor. He was at his desk, frowning at his monitor. He looked up and smiled when she knocked. "Catherine. Come in."

Seth's office was a little smaller than Call-Me-Lance's, a regular square instead of an L, with no room for anything like exercise equipment, but it had the better view. On the same side of the building as the balcony, he could see Parliament Hill.

"Have a seat. What can I do for you?"

Catherine settled into the chair on the other side of his desk. She'd been dreading this conversation. "This is going to be difficult. Please know that I wouldn't bring this up if it wasn't serious."

Seth sobered. "I understand."

Ok. Here we go. "Mr. MacCallan has been acting towards me in an improper manner, consistently, over the past two weeks." Past three weeks, if one considered his reprehensible behaviour of the first week, but she wasn't going to go into that. It would muddy her argument, maybe cause Seth to think she was making everything up because she thought Call-Me-Lance hadn't been nice enough to her in the beginning.

"How so?"

He didn't appear shocked, which was a little disquieting, but at least he wasn't tossing her out of his office without listening to her.

She had planned her words in advance. "While I have been in many workplaces in which the employees were given gifts, I made it clear from the beginning that I didn't want such gifts. I didn't want the NAC ticket. The flowers were highly inappropriate, given what red roses usually mean."

Seth expressed no surprise upon learning the identity of the person who had given her the flowers. "Lance is a generous man. Always has been."

All right. He wanted to interpret his friend's actions in the best light possible. She could understand that. "From the first time he asked me to socialise with him, I made it clear I didn't want to. He's asked me out again and again, even though I've been saying no from the very beginning. I believe he had Samantha arrange for me to join him for drinks last Friday while deliberately causing me to think he wouldn't be there."

"A group of you went out and everyone told me they had a great time."

It was early Monday morning. Everyone had had a chance to tell him about their Friday night? Why would they even choose to do so? They had come to work and before they went to their desks they had all stopped by Seth's office to tell him how fabulous Friday had been?

The red flags were going up.

"He came to my apartment on Saturday expecting to take me on a picnic, and when I said no, he grabbed my arm and tried to drag me to his car." There was no positive interpretation to put on that.

Seth chuckled. *Chuckled!* "He doesn't know his own strength. Once I made a joke at his expense, and he punched me in the arm. It was all meant in fun, of course, but I had a bruise for a week."

A cold weight was growing in the pit of her stomach. "He called me into his office this morning and he wasn't wearing a shirt. Or pants."

"We don't have a formal atmosphere here. It stifles creativity. Has anyone told you about our Polar Bear Club?"

Did Seth seriously expect her to believe Call-Me-Lance regularly called employees into his office and greeted them in nothing but a pair of shorts?

She pulled out the big guns. "He told me he wanted to have sex with me."

"Were those his exact words?"

Seth had asked that question before. She was sure of it. "Not his exact words, no."

Seth shrugged. "A misunderstanding."

Yeah, Seth knew exactly what kind of person Call-Me-Lance was, and he didn't give a rat's ass. There would be no help for her there.

He had a daughter. Catherine knew her name. She had seen it in the emails congratulating Seth upon his daughter's acceptance into Queen's. Catherine wanted to say something snarky, maybe that she hoped his daughter didn't encounter any difficulty in the engineering department, which had had some scandals in the past, its male students making fun of rape.

But no, bringing his daughter into the discussion would be a cheap shot.

Besides, if Seth said something along the lines that his daughter would never experience any such problems because she was a good girl, Catherine would want to hit him.

Still, he had a daughter and yet had no problem with the way Call-Me-Lance abused women. What kind of personality enabled a father to do that?

Catherine smiled tightly. "Thank you for your time." She rose to her feet.

"No trouble at all. Don't hesitate to come back if you need anything."

The bald-faced insincerity made her want to vomit.

She had anticipated various reactions from Seth. Anger. The refusal to accept her words. At the very best, a reluctant promise to look into it. That he'd been aware of Call-Me-Lance's behaviour and didn't care floored her.

Was that how he had treated all the C and C employees who had complained about Call-Me-Lance?

No more little emails saying hello and good-bye to Seth.

Catherine went to Sandy's office.

Sandy gave her a blank look upon hearing Catherine's request. "We don't have a sexual harassment policy," she said, sounding astonished to be asked.

Catherine was so appalled that all she could do was parrot, "You don't have a sexual harassment policy."

"We don't need one. We all get along here."

Had Catherine stepped into some weird updated version of Stepford?

Wondering if her question would be kept within those four walls, she thanked Sandy for her time and walked back to her workspace. She sat in the chair. She stared at the monitor.

What business the size of C and C didn't have a sexual harassment policy? For the look of it, if no other reason?

Perhaps she had been naïve, but she hadn't expected to get absolutely no help at all, to have it made so clear that no one would even think of doing something.

Work was beyond her at the moment. She logged off and went to the elevator.

She wanted to call Lina, but she refused to freak out on her busy friend yet again. She was an adult. She could handle this.

She went to the food court and looked at the options. She wanted to eat something to try to calm down, but nothing was appealing to her.

Did everyone at C and C know that Call-Me-Lance was a sexually harassing psycho and just not care? Even the women?

Did they see him as their ticket to wealth and consider that sufficient motive to shield him?

Were they too afraid to do anything?

What was she going to do?

She still had one more person to talk to, a person who would be interested in helping her, so she could relax.

Ha!

Friday was her last day. There would be no more Saturday encounters. She would say no to everything. She would be fine.

She checked her yahoo account on her phone and found an email from her friend confirming she could meet for lunch on Wednesday. That made Catherine feel a little better.

She went to the coffee shop and ordered a large caffè mocha with whipped cream. Scooping the cream up with her index finger and popping it into her mouth did soothe her nerves a little. It didn't take long until she felt ready to go back up.

She attacked the C and C emails. By then, she knew the timing of the rising, the coasting, and the falling of In-Ect. She knew nothing happened between September of 2010 and June of 2012, and she knew nothing important happened after January of 2014. She was able to swiftly recognise and dismiss irrelevant email threads she'd encountered before. While technically she was reading every email, she was doing a lot of skimming and she got through folders fairly quickly.

Call-Me-Lance left her alone until 3:28, at which point he plunked before her a solo cup from the coffee shop. There was a lid on the cup, but from the smell and the letters scratched on the side, Catherine knew it was a caffè mocha with whipped cream.

She looked up at him, incredulous. "Did you follow me?"

Sure, she had suspected he might have spent some time watching her, but to have it confirmed added a whole new level of creepy.

And if he thought everything she did was an attempt to be sexually alluring, knowing he'd watched her eat whipped cream with her finger, knowing what he probably thought of it, made her want to cringe.

"No," he said with a smile. "I know you. I bet I know you better than you know yourself."

"After three weeks and not a single genuine conversation," she said sarcastically.

He smirked. "The secret of my success is knowing what people want before they know they want it. And giving it to them."

"I am literally nauseated right now." She picked up the cup and set it back down on the table in front of him. "I've had enough of this and I don't want any more."

"I have a feeling you've been taught you have no right to ask for more. I consider it my duty to help you break those chains."

She couldn't help it. She laughed in his face.

And, oh, he didn't like that. He stepped back, his eyes narrowed, and for a second she thought he was going to say something vicious.

Instead, he pasted on a smile. "You poor thing, you don't even know you're wearing chains."

Apparently under the delusion his words were a thought-provoking verbal blow, he turned to leave.

"Don't forget your coffee," she told him.

"I'll leave it with you. You'll want it later." He strutted off like a pigeon, pleased with himself.

She rolled her eyes and threw the coffee in the trash in the lunchroom.

At least he didn't bug her for the rest of the day. That was something.

Chapter Twenty-Five

Tuesday, October 6, 2015
Arrived approximately 8:49 am.

There was an email from Ms. Levitt waiting in Catherine's C and C account.

Dear Ms. Aherne:
This is incredible work. I am rarely provided
with so much information in such an organised
document. There is no need to change your
process. I look forward to your final draft.
Yours very truly,
Dani B. Levitt

What a handy sentiment to have put into the written word. Catherine forwarded the email to her yahoo account.

Then she hit the employee folders.

She had had no real hope for a Call-Me-Lance-free day, but it was still a disappointment when she got an email from him at 11:29.

Please come to my office.

At least he was dressed, and he was sitting at his desk.

"Aherne is an Irish name," he announced as soon as she stepped through his door.

Which she left open. "Yes, I'm aware of that."

"Have you ever thought of exploring your roots?"

"Of course."

"Dublin is a fantastic city," he said with confidence, apparently assuming Catherine had no way of knowing that herself. "The Trinity campus is beautiful. And this is something you'll appreciate; it's said a former provost of the school swore women would be allowed as students over his dead body, and that he's buried on campus, and the female students enjoy - "

"Stepping over his dead body," Catherine interrupted. "Yes, I took the tour."

Call-Me-Lance sat back in his chair. "You took the tour," he said flatly.

"Dublin *is* a great city, but I don't know, I felt a stronger connection to Rosslare." While Catherine was in no way an outdoorsy person, the peacefulness of open natural spaces was soothing. "Though that might have been because I was staying at a fabulous resort at the time." And she had gone horseback riding on the beach, all by herself. She wouldn't tell him that, though. It wouldn't jibe with her claim to have been turned off riding. "Donegal has a wild beauty that is somehow invigorating." But it was too far from everything else. That bus ride to Belfast; oy. "And then there's Kinsale. It's a unique experience to visit an ordinary person who lives in an ordinary small house that just happens to be older than Canada." That *had* been odd. It was one thing to visit such buildings as a tourist, to pay for a quick look around, but to spend a week in one, sleeping and reading and cooking on the stove and living normally, that was different. At times, she had laid her hands on the stones and wondered who had been living in that house in 1867. "And it's a tiny city with what felt like a million pubs."

Call-Me-Lance grinned, undaunted. "But have you gone first class?"

"My aunt worked for British Airways back when the job had amazing perks and upgrades weren't so hard to come by. Everyone in my family has flown first class. Is that all?"

"We could ask Lina to come with us," he suggested jovially. "She's quite a looker and threesomes are wild."

The air was knocked out of her. For a moment, she literally couldn't breathe. She found herself at her workspace without remembering how she got there. She sent a text to Lina.

He knows who you are.

She mechanically went through emails until she heard her phone ring. She rushed out to reception and went to the end farther from Nancy, crowding close to the window, not caring how strange it looked to Nancy or anyone else who might wander into the otherwise empty area.

"What the freaking hell?" Lina shouted.

"I know," Catherine responded miserably. "I know. I'm sorry."

"You better be doing something," Lina warned her, anger in her tone.

"I am. I'm seeing a lawyer tomorrow. Nalla Dillon. I've told you about her before."

"Why can't you do something now?"

"I tried. Remember Seth, the allegedly nice one? I talked to him about this and it's obvious he knows exactly what MacCallan's like and doesn't care. And this place doesn't have a sexual harassment policy."

"That's impossible," Lina said shortly.

"If they do, they're not admitting it to me."

"Leave."

"I'm not letting him win."

"How is he losing? You're tense all the time. When you're not tense, you're terrified. You're afraid to use the washrooms on that floor, for Christ's sake. You were afraid to go to the Market last Saturday. When was the last time you wrote something? The D&D campaign doesn't count."

Not since she'd walked into C and C. Usually she started something new while her editor was working on her current manuscript. Nothing was coming to her.

"He is breaking the law," Lina reminded her. "And he's getting away with it. And you're letting him, for the sake of a stupid temp job."

"I will be done on Friday. All leaving three days early will accomplish is failure. I will be destroying my reputation with Fast Act all by myself."

"Not if you tell them why."

"That's why I'm talking to Nalla, so I can make my complaint to Fast Act in the right way. I'm not going to blunder about blindly. The best way to approach them is in an organised fashion, because I have only one chance to talk to them before he does. I have to put my best foot forward right off the bat, because if I have to change anything after he responds, it will weaken my whole case."

"This isn't a trial," Lina pointed out in a tone of frustration.

"But it could turn into one, so I might as well begin as I mean to go on. It's the best way to make sure he faces some consequences. And maybe stop him from doing it again to someone else."

After a long pause, Lina said, "If I see him, I'm calling the police."

"Yes. And I will support you with everything I have."

Lina said nothing.

"I'm so sorry, Lina."

"Whatever." Lina disconnected.

Anger and resentment towards Call-Me-Lance rose in Catherine, and her grip tightened on the phone. She threw it into her purse to avoid damaging it.

She couldn't believe he'd dragged Lina into it. Was her friend in danger? Or was he simply using another way to frighten Catherine?

Interesting seduction technique.

It didn't matter what his motive was. It didn't change what she had to do. Nalla would be able to tell her what kind of information she needed to take to Fast Act and how to present it. Cross every t and dot every i. So that, if Fast Act did refuse to do anything, Catherine could demonstrate that the failing was theirs, not hers, at the next step. Whatever that next step might be.

But that Call-Me-Lance had gone after Lina at all, for any reason, was infuriating.

Catherine took a few deep breaths, lowered her shoulders, and went back to her workspace.

At 3:13, Call-Me-Lance slunk close. "Check your yahoo account."

She didn't. She kept going through the C and C folders.

When she did get home and check her yahoo account, she thought Call-Me-Lance had merely taken another opportunity to yank her chain, as she found nothing but the usual sorts of things from friends and family. Then she went to her spam box to empty it, and something from an idiot calling himself yourstruly69 jumped out at her.

"God," she said with disdain. She didn't want to open it, but she knew she had to, to know what he was up to.

The subject was a smiley face. There was no text, just pictures of a suite in a resort in Rosslare.

She shifted the cursor to delete the email, but she stopped. Instead, she printed it. Another addition to her binder.

And she read C and C emails.

Chapter Twenty-Six

"There's nothing you can do," Nalla said, crossing her arms and sitting back in her chair.

"What do you mean there's nothing I can do?" Catherine demanded. Loudly. Too loudly. She glanced at all of the filled tables around them, crowded into the food court of a building three skyscrapers away from the one that held C and C. It was noisy, she doubted anyone had heard her, but she leaned over the table and continued in a lower voice. "How can all of this be useless?" She tapped the binder on the table. "I know he's breaking the law."

"He is," Nalla agreed. "He should be charged, and in an ideal world, your evidence would be enough for a judge to at least consider convicting him of something. But you know we don't live in that world. What he's doing isn't bad enough. From the sounds of it, he's shown some care with his word choice. He hasn't threatened you with anything other than firing you, and some could say that at that time you weren't doing what you had been hired to do. It could be claimed that the arm across your shoulder was merely a sign of being friendly. People grab each other's arms when they disagree without it meaning anything. He could claim you told him about Lina, that you invited him to your apartment. It can all be explained away, and from the sounds of it, he's got over forty people who'll say what a great guy he is to work for."

Catherine slumped back in her chair. She'd known she didn't have a slam dunk case, but she thought she'd had something. "I don't understand how he can treat everyone else so well and treat me like trash."

"That's how some people are. They value some and despise others. But it could be .... You know that expression, in the land of the blind, the one-eyed man is king."

"Of course."

"In a culture in which most employers treat their employees like shit, it's not hard to look like a prince. A company making those kinds of profits with a staff that size, how much effort and money goes into pizza on Thursdays, a few catered parties a year, and that polar bear stuff? What kind of salaries and benefits are they getting? That's where you'll get a real picture."

"No clue," Catherine muttered. "Their salaries are the only thing they don't talk about in their emails."

"Regardless, he's developed an environment that encourages loyalty. And that makes sense. Everyone should do it. But isn't it handy that it also creates a whole team of people willing to protect him when an outsider attacks? You said everyone thinks you're sleeping with him."

"Yes," Catherine answered bitterly.

"There you go. A temp makes a play for the boss, he refuses or dumps her, she tries to destroy his good name out of spite."

A tale as old as time. "But what about civil court? The standard of proof is lower."

"What are your damages? You're a temp with no reasonable expectation of continued employment. All of the agencies could drop you and claim the work isn't there. Bad economy and all that. Even if you could convince a judge that MacCallan deliberately and successfully caused you to lose income, it would be for an amount so low, it wouldn't even be worth a small claims court proceeding."

Catherine opened the binder and fanned the pages. All that information, and it meant nothing.

"The best case scenario," Nalla continued, "is that MacCallan admits to someone that, yes, maybe he stepped over the line, but only with the best of intentions, honest. Someone will wag their finger at him and tell him to create a sexual harassment policy. He will promise to do so, and that will be the end of that. Are you prepared to endure the time, stress, money, and damage to your reputation for that?"

Sometimes Catherine hated life.

"I'm sorry, I know this sucks. He's a bastard and you shouldn't have to go through this. But I'm telling you what I'd tell any stranger who came into my office with the same set of facts. Chalk it up to a bad experience and move on." Nalla checked her watch. "I'm sorry. I've got to go."

"Yeah." Catherine tried to claw out of her fog of despair. "Thanks for looking at this. I know it's obnoxious to ask you for legal advice on the fly."

Nalla smiled at her sympathetically and patted her arm before leaving.

Catherine put her face in her hands. Nothing. Absolutely nothing. She couldn't believe it.

Right then, finishing the job didn't seem so important. Staying at C and C meant submitting to Call-Me-Lance's abuse. Yet what would she say to Fast Act if she quit? Nalla had agreed that the temp agency would be more interested in keeping a client than a temp. And if Catherine deserted a job before it was finished, they wouldn't want to give her another one.

Catherine could probably come up with some convincing excuse, but that lie would also serve to protect Call-Me-Lance. She would see her reputation trashed before she would do that.

She had to go back.

When she threw out her untouched lunch, she almost threw the binder out with it. Instead, she took the binder back to her car and returned to C and C to read emails.

By the time she received a request from Call-Me-Lance to join him in his office, she was numb. Sure, she would go. Why not? What difference would it make?

When she stepped through the door, he tossed something at her, and without thought she caught it in her left hand. It was a velvet jewellery box. She opened it, because what else was she going to do?

It was a tennis bracelet, she believed, though she'd never seen one in real life. A string of what looked to her untrained eyes to be fairly large diamonds, set in white gold or platinum.

He really thought he could buy her. He thought he could denigrate and threaten and stalk and harass her and then just flash some cash and she'd become eager and willing. The idiocy of it was oddly invigorating.

"You can wear it when we go to Ireland," he said.

"We're not going to Ireland."

"Didn't my email tempt you?"

"I didn't get an email from you. I did get an email from a pathetic loser calling himself yourstruly69, but I deleted that without reading it." He frowned, but she charged on. "Are these Canadian diamonds?"

He blinked, perhaps caught off guard by the abrupt change of subject. "What?"

"I wear only Canadian diamonds." She'd never worn diamonds, even when she could afford them, because the diamond industry was a racket, but if she were to buy a diamond, she'd fork over the insane pile of dollars needed to buy a Canadian one. "It's the best way to be sure they're conflict free." There were scenes from *Blood Diamond* she would never be able to forget. The men getting their arms chopped off. The young boy grinning with delight as he sprayed terrified villagers with bullets.

"Yes, they're Canadian."

"Where's the certificate?"

He raised an eyebrow. "You have to see how much it costs before you decide whether you like it?"

Of course he was the type to assume everyone was avaricious. "Not the receipt, the certificate that says exactly where the diamonds were mined."

"I must have mislaid it," he said smoothly.

"Ah. Too bad." She snapped the box closed and tossed it back, but onto the desk, not into his hands. It bounced and he had to move quickly to stop it from flying off and hitting the floor. "It's nice, though. Maybe you have an elderly relative you can give it to."

"Don't be so pleased with yourself," he warned her as she left his office. "I'm good at this."

No, he wasn't. And it was odd. Lina had been right, it was like he was going down a checklist, or referring to a manual. The lack of creativity his behaviour implied made Catherine wonder if he was the guy who lured in clients and money while everyone else had the ideas.

Lina. What was Catherine going to do about Lina? She'd expected to be able to tell her friend the good news Nalla was supposed to give her.

She didn't think Lina was in danger. For Call-Me-Lance to expand his scope of harassment to an outsider would not only be an extremely risky move on his part, as two victims had far more weight than one, but it would be a drastic elevation of his campaign of assault. It didn't fall in line with his process up to date, which had been to take relatively small steps at a time. He thought he still had two days and two weeks to play his game. He might engage in drastic tactics in what he anticipated would be her last week, but not yet.

No, nothing would happen to Lina before Catherine ended the job on Friday. She was sure of it. Almost 100% sure.

She wouldn't tell Lina what Nalla had said. Not yet. No reason to worry her.

But Call-Me-Lance's latest clumsy attempt to suggest Catherine should take up prostitution had woken her brain up.

She worked her way through more folders, learning nothing except that two employees had been cheating on their wives with each other.

She left at approximately 5:04.

After her supper, she tried to read through more emails, but she was distracted.

What would *she* do if a potential client came to her for legal advice with her set of facts? How would she represent that person in court? What statutes and case law would she need? What terminology? What was the best way to craft the argument?

Nalla had been able to spare her only twenty minutes. The lawyer hadn't had a chance to thoroughly look at the binder or give the problem a lot of thought.

Stalking, sexual harassment, and assault. The possibilities in criminal and civil court. Workplace sexual harassment was, she thought, purely in the purview of the Human Rights Commission, but she wasn't sure. She needed to explore all of the options. If she reported Call-Me-Lance to Fast Act, he might go after her for defamation and slander. If Fast Act dropped her because of Call-Me-Lance, Catherine didn't know what the next step was, Nalla hadn't had time to cover that, but Catherine could find out.

Catherine had a LexisNexis account, a knack for online research, and a thirst for vengeance. What else did she need?

First search; legal definitions. The website of the Ontario Human Rights Commission had a ton of them.

Chapter Twenty-Seven

That Thursday was the best day Catherine had had at C and C. Call-Me-Lance didn't make an appearance, and no one else bothered her. Seth didn't even try one of his pseudo-friendly chats.

The five days spent creating the separate folders, while tedious, were paying off, and Catherine was whipping through the emails. As most of them didn't refer to In-Ect at all, and only a few had been sent to or received from Under-Ware, there was little to add to her report to Levitt. She was tempted to skip the employees who had come and gone before June of 2012 and those who had been hired after January of 2014, but no. Every single frakking email.

She would finish on time, either way.

Left approximately 5:09.

There was a bounce to her steps as she took the elevator down and walked the five blocks to her parking lot. *Almost done, almost done, almost done.*

She went to the booth and held her ticket out to the attendant. "The green Yaris, please."

"That's not the one she wants."

She jumped, noticeably, at Call-Me-Lance's words. He was right behind her.

What the hell? He had not been following her. She was sure of it.

Except she wasn't sure of it. She hadn't been paying attention, too happy over a Call-Me-Lance-free day and the light at the end of the tunnel. And the sidewalks were crowded. She would have driven herself crazy trying to figure out who was walking behind her.

She wanted to punch him in the face. She knew how to do it properly.

She had suffered more violent impulses in the past few weeks than in all of the time since her ill-fated attempt to live with a boyfriend.

"She wants the silver Mustang convertible."

Call-Me-Lance didn't have a ticket, because of course he wasn't required to conform to the normal operating procedure of the parking lot. He held out a key.

The attendant accepted Call-Me-Lance's word over Catherine's and took the key.

"No, I want the green Yaris." She spoke more loudly and more firmly and was ignored.

Grinning, the attendant left the booth and walked toward a silver convertible that, aside from the colour, was exactly like Call-Me-Lance's.

"You need to learn how versatile convertibles are," Call-Me-Lance declared.

"Where's my car?" she demanded.

"I have a mechanic who'll keep her purring like a kitten."

"Where's my car?"

"You might be surprised how far back the seats go."

"Where's my car!" she shouted.

Call-Me-Lance stared at her as though she were the one who was behaving badly. The parking attendant stopped a metre from the convertible and turned to gape at her.

"If you had my car towed somewhere, I'll call the cops and report you for theft." The police might not care about what Nalla had referred to as minor sexual harassment, but they got interested when property was stolen.

"Calm down," Call-Me-Lance ordered with disdain. "Your piece of shit is still here."

"The green Yaris," she told the attendant, holding out her ticket. He took it with a look of confusion and went back to the booth for her keys.

"You're quite the ungrateful bitch," Call-Me-Lance commented as the attendant found Catherine's car in a mess of them at the back of the lot. "When I return this, I'm going to lose a fortune."

Yeah, that was totally her fault. "Don't you have another victim to give it to?"

He snorted. "Victim. If that's the kind of advice the lawyer you met for lunch yesterday is giving you, I hope you're not paying for her time."

Catherine knew she should be disturbed to learn that he had followed her yesterday, that he seemed to be following her all the time despite having a business to run, and perhaps the fact that she was finishing the next day was giving her a false sense of security, but her primary reaction was the thought that Nalla's opinion of the case might change once she learned Call-Me-Lance was trying to drag her into it, too. Catherine, Lina, and Nalla represented three stalking victims. He was a serial stalker. "On the contrary, the advice she gave me was … motivating."

"You didn't seem so motivated at the time."

"We both know appearances can be deceptive."

He glowered at her.

She grinned back, angry and entertained all at the same time.

The attendant pulled the Yaris in front of her and got out. "Have a good evening," she said to Call-Me-Lance as she settled into the driver's seat, slamming the door closed before he could say anything.

That had been fun.

When she got home, she spent half an hour in the exercise room, showered and ate a light supper, plugged in the coffee maker, and turned on her laptop.

At 2:11 am, she finished putting the final touches on her report to Levitt.

Chapter Twenty-Eight

Friday, October 9, 2015
Arrived approximately 8:29 am.

Catherine didn't send the report to Levitt right away. She didn't want to warn anyone that she was leaving that day. Instead, she went online to follow up on the list of former and disgruntled C and C employees. Why not? It was a way to pass the time.

No one talked to her, so she got a lot done. She didn't see Call-Me-Lance, but she didn't expect to be left alone by him all day. She didn't care. It was the last day, and she'd done her job.

It wasn't an employee of C and C who proved to be interesting. It was Wade Anderson, the former Under-Ware employee who hadn't been on the list she'd been given on her first day. And what he was doing was very interesting indeed. She kept looking and started a new memo.

Call-Me-Lance came in at 2:59, taking the path by her workspace and trailing a finger over her neck as he whispered, "You have no idea what I have planned for you this weekend."

Insult her one day and expect her to have forgotten it the next. Truly baffling behaviour. She was tempted to go back to school and major in psychology just to try to figure out how people like him could exist.

At 4:31, she printed the memo about Wade Anderson.

At 4:35, she drafted a short letter and printed it.

At 4:40, she filled out her Fast Act hour report, anticipating she would be leaving shortly after 5:00. She made a copy.

At 4:45, she sent an email to Ms. Levitt.

Dear Ms. Levitt:
Please find attached my final report.
Sincerely,

Catherine Aherne

At 4:55, she sent a mass email to everyone at C and C.

Hi everyone:
Today is my last day. Working with you has been a great experience.
All the best,
Catherine

At 4:58, she got an email from Call-Me-Lance.

My office. Now.

She saluted the monitor. "Sir, yes, sir." She logged off and went to Call-Me-Lance's office, taking the Anderson memo and her purse with her.

He was pacing in the right part of his office, his eyes narrowed, jaw tight, fists clenched. Although that part of the L had only the chair and the two couches, there wasn't a lot of room to stalk about. It made him look hemmed in, not threatening.

He stopped and growled at her, standing too closely in front of her. "What do you think you're doing, leaving mid-contract?"

His voice was low. He wouldn't be heard in the bullpen. She wondered at his attempt at discretion. If he shouted, all the others would hear was the boss chastising a temp who was leaving, and they would believe it was because she'd done a bad job. Or that she was causing a scene after being dumped by him. Why would he care about that? Would the fact that he was shouting shock them? Would it make them think he wasn't such a great guy after all?

She resisted the urge to step back and shrugged. "I'm finished. I sent everything to Ms. Levitt. There's no reason to stay."

"My complaint to Fast Act about your shoddy work will be made by 5:30."

She didn't doubt it, and that worried her, but she had prepared for this and kept her tone calm as she said, "Good luck with that. I finished the job early, despite getting an extra assignment. I've logged extra hours in my Fast Act report. I got an email from your lawyer about how great my work is."

"An email to your work account. That can disappear."

"Deliberately eliminating evidence is called spoliation. Luckily, I forwarded the email to my yahoo account."

He hesitated before saying, "The hours on the Fast Act reports are taken on faith. It's easy to say you fudged them."

"The fact that I so frequently sent an email to Seth to say hi as soon as I got in and sent an email to say bye before leaving proves I had a habit of coming early and leaving late." Of course, they could make those disappear, too. She hadn't forwarded them to her account. Sloppy thinking on her part, damn it.

"I know you were taking work home. That's a violation of the non-disclosure agreement you signed. Lawsuits are started over things like that." He smirked, obviously thinking he had her over a barrel.

"It's not a violation of the non-disclosure agreement, because the non-disclosure agreement is crap. It only stops me from sharing information with outside parties, and I didn't. Nothing about taking anything off the premises. Did you lot get a lawyer to draft your documents when you started this company or did you just copy and paste stuff from the internet? I hate to think what your by-laws look like."

He gaped at her.

She was sure he was usually much more on the ball, even when that ball was delivered with a curve, but this was an area of knowledge she had that he lacked, and she'd had it on the brain since Wednesday night. "And if you do trash me to Fast Act, or sue me, think of all my options for a counter-suit. Stalking, assault, sexual harassment, defamation."

Recovering his confidence, he flicked his hand. "You have no proof of anything."

Oh, but she did. Weak proof, but advocacy was all about making weak evidence look strong, conveying with tone, body language, and every word that the only possible interpretation of events was the one she was providing.

"There's the surveillance camera at my apartment building. It demonstrates that you came to my home, assumed a threatening posture, and assaulted me." Though she didn't know if that video still existed. She doubted the superintendents had the means to hold on to the videos for very long. "While anything Lina has to say would be hearsay, the fact that I immediately contacted her after some of your more outrageous stunts means she might be allowed to testify to my state of mind. Like that I thought you were an abusive ass from the very first day, and that this isn't about me making everything up afterwards because of some imagined slight. Or punishing you for dumping me."

His face flushed and he raised his hand, his fingers curling as though he meant to grab her.

She stepped back before he could touch her. "And then there are my notes."

He snorted. "No judge is going to care about some chick's diary."

"On the contrary, judges give a lot of weight to contemporaneous notes. One of my clients was charged with over twenty counts of assault based on nothing more than his ex's diary. No witnesses. No medical records. No other evidence of any kind. And judges give even more weight to notes written by people in professions in which taking regular notes is the norm. Cops. Medical experts. Lawyers."

He looked at her purse.

Catherine didn't know what he was thinking, so she added, "I've made copies, of course."

He could run everything she had said by a lawyer, get a different interpretation of the events, but not by 5:30, and probably not before Monday. If she could stall him a little, the delay might make his accusations look weaker.

"It doesn't matter what evidence you think you have," Call-Me-Lance sneered. "No one will believe you. Everyone loves me. Not just here, but everywhere. Did you see all of those industry awards?"

"I admit it would be tough," she conceded, "but given recent events, people no longer find it quite so hard to believe successful, charismatic men might be abusing people. Behind the scenes. And you know, I've read some emails that make it clear your employees might not love you as much as you think." Everyone who had written those emails was gone, so she didn't feel badly about throwing them to the wolves. The idea of Call-Me-Lance combing through five years worth of emails trying to find the ones slagging him off was deeply satisfying. "The whole time I've been here, I haven't seen a single person playing with any of the toys you've got sprinkled about. Are your underlings really allowed to use them or are they all for show? Something to make outsiders think this is a free and creative environment when you give them a tour."

After a moment of gnashing his teeth, he spat, "It was a bet. A bet I could get you into bed. I wouldn't have given you a second look if it wasn't for that. I hate losers."

Ah. While she hadn't considered the possibility of a bet, it didn't surprise her. She was aware some people engaged in that kind of infantile behaviour, and it explained his actions. "Then I guess you won't be able to look in the mirror for a while. Maybe you should see a therapist about that. And all of your other severe mental health issues." He opened his mouth to speak, but she kept on trucking, holding up her memo. "This is some information about Wade Anderson, a former Under-Ware employee who was involved in the discussions about In-Ect and whom you failed to put on your list." She emphasised the word 'failed.' "He and some pals started their own software company and they've just launched a Kickstarter campaign. They have plans for an online social networking site that looks a lot more like In-Ect than Circle Route does. You might want to look into that." She turned to toss the memo onto his desk and then turned back to Call-Me-Lance. "I hope it was a Duke and Duke bet."

He looked baffled. "What?"

"Only a dollar. Because you lost." She grinned at him. "You lost hard." She practically twirled out of the office.

"It was a quarter!" he shouted after her. "And you're probably a lesbian!"

Catherine couldn't stop smiling. She had no doubt Call-Me-Lance wouldn't admit to his dudebro followers that he'd failed. Maybe he would claim the unexpected loss of two weeks violated the terms of the bet. Maybe he would flat out lie and tell them she'd let him screw her. She didn't care. The two of them knew he had failed, and that was good enough for her.

Next stop, human resources.

Sandy was there, and she accepted Catherine's Fast Act report with confusion. "I don't understand why you're leaving early," she said.

While Catherine hadn't expected Sandy to refer to her request for a copy of the non-existent sexual harassment policy, she thought it was hilarious that the HR agent was trying to pretend Catherine hadn't asked for it at all. To Catherine's face.

"I finished early."

"I thought you were told we were hoping to give you more work."

Everyone at C and C was deluded. "No one said that was a certainty, and another opportunity came up." That opportunity being freedom.

"We'll miss you."

Catherine managed to keep herself from rolling her eyes yet again. She was worried about straining them. "Here's my security card. And could you sign this, please?" She held out the letter she had printed.

"What is it?"

"An acknowledgement that I gave you the card. To avoid any misunderstandings later. I'm anal."

With an expression of irritation, Sandy signed the letter and returned it.

"Thank you so much." Catherine refolded the letter and put it back into her purse. "Have a good weekend."

"You, too," Sandy said faintly.

Catherine pulled open the glass door between the bullpen and reception for the last time. She strolled to the elevator and pushed the button. "Bye, Nancy," she said cheerfully.

"I'm sorry you're leaving us so soon."

Catherine couldn't tell whether the other woman was being sincere or not. She had always seemed nice, but Catherine had never had a conversation with her. And normally she would feel bad about that, upon realising it, but the woman willingly worked at C and C, so Catherine didn't give a damn. "That's the nature of being a temp. We come and we go."

"Maybe we'll have a chance to bring you back in the future." *Geez, these people are weird.* "Maybe."

When Catherine got into the elevator, she did a little dance. When others got into the elevator, they gave her strange looks because she was grinning like a maniac. When she got to the first floor, she wanted to fling her arms out, spin around, and shout, "Wheeee!" so everyone could see how happy she was.

She didn't.

It would be a weekend of celebration, starting with filling her cupboards with all of the luxurious food she was usually too sensible to buy. She would take a giant chocolate trifle to Lina to say *mea culpa*. She would finish her D&D campaign.

She ran around downtown trying to hit every business she could before everything closed for the day. The bakery, the butcher, the cheese shop, the chocolate shop. And the liquor store, of course. She ignored the prices. That was what credit cards were for.

And as she ran around, she decided she would report Call-Me-Lance everywhere she could - Fast Act, the police department, the Human Rights Commission - and let the chips fall where they would. She was aware that in her euphoria, she might be dismissing the consequences of her actions too recklessly, but she didn't care. She knew if she didn't report him, it wouldn't be long before she regretted it. And maybe she wouldn't be the first to file a complaint against him, and she would be supporting someone else's story. Or perhaps, in a few years, someone with a more solid case would step forward, and the evidence Catherine had provided would make that case even stronger.

It had happened before.

It was after six before she got to her car, parked in a different lot than the one she'd used before. She turned the ignition, a song blaring out of the radio. Catherine sang along with the chorus as she pulled out of the lot.

"Since you been gone, I can breathe for the first time!

I'm so movin' on, yeah yeah!"

She turned west and had to pull down the sun visor. The sunset was awfully bright.

Other books written by this author include the following:

Resenting the Hero
The Hero Strikes Back
Heroes Adrift
Heroes at Risk
Heroes Return
Heroes at Odds
Heroes' Reward

The author keeps a blog at moiraj.livejournal.com